Lost Memories FOUND HOPE

This book is dedicated to all those
in the thick of Alzheimer's caregiving. With Love.

www.facebook.com/LostMemoriesFoundHope
www.MichelleSpray.com

by Michelle Spray

Lost Memories Found Hope
A Granddaughter's Story of Love throughout Alzheimer's
by Michelle Spray ©2018, ©2020

Published by
Book Shelf
1083 East Main St.
Suite C4, PMB 111
Torrington, CT 06790
www.MichelleSpray.com

Although many parts of this story are true, this is a work of fiction. All people, names, places, businesses, events and incidents are either the products of the author's imagination or used in a fictitious manner. Any resemblance to actual persons, living or dead, or actual events is purely coincidental.

Editor: Natalie Bates
Cover Photo: © Tracy Weed 2018
Cover Design: © Michelle Spray 2018

ISBN-13: 978-0-692-17384-8
ISBN-10: 0-692-17384-6

Contents

Alzheimer's Poetry

"Courage is going forward into a place where you cannot see the destination, putting one foot in front of the other while pulling a 1,400 pound sled. Isn't that what we do daily with our loved ones? We don't know what the day will be like when we rise in the morning. We've lost our own futures — if that isn't a 1,400 pound sled we're pulling, I don't know what is. And yet, we do it. One step at a time, one foot in front of the other. We whine a little bit (or a lot) along the way. We seek companionship from others who know our plight. But we get out of bed, and sometimes, that is the biggest act of courage for a caregiver. And having others to help you pull that sled? That's God's gift." – Angela Lunde, Alzheimer's Caregiving Newsletter, April 5th, 2011

- *Chapter One* -

Growing up, Jillian never went more than a couple of days without being at Grandma's house. Grandma's was the place for homemade dinners, complete with bread to dunk and sauce to wipe from their chins. It was the place for hugs, treats, overnights, and peace. She didn't even mind being quiet while Grandma watched her "story" at two o'clock every day as long as she could be in the same room.

Where was Jillian's mother? No one knew. Maybe she was getting a manicure. Maybe she was getting her hair cut, her pride and joy; a sleek, fire-red bob. Maybe she was buying makeup. She never left the house without her "face on" and she wore lots of it. Maybe she was gambling at the Jai Alai where Jillian had spent lots of time. Jillian knew what a trifecta was, which players were good, and which players to heckle; although she knew to keep her mouth shut. The truth was that Jillian didn't much care where her mother was, as long as she could spend time with Grandma.

When Jillian had to stay home sick from school, she would be dropped off at Grandma's house. Sometimes Grandma would drive her to the store so she could "give the germs away" to someone else and not get Grandpa sick. But most days, she'd sit quietly on Grandma's yellow chair with her legs straight out, too short to fold over the edge. Grandma cultivated her love of writing while Grandpa worked in the yard. Jillian was especially excited about a poem she wrote and illustrated one day about a ladybug. She was in the middle of showing Grandma when her mother walked in.

"Uh-huh." Her mother dismissed her, shoving her out the

door when she tried to show her the project that took her hours. "Get in the car."

"Mommy," Jillian tried to hold back the tears, "I forgot something inside." Jillian ran back into the house to confide in Grandma.

"Mommy hates it."

"She doesn't hate it Jillie-Bean. She's just … busy."

Grandma pulled her in for a quick snuggle and Jillian wiped her tears in Grandma's apron … for the millionth time.

Grandma was always there. She would drop off sandwiches to elementary school when Jillian's mother forgot to make lunch or when the nuns ran out of peanut butter. Grandma's sandwiches were the best, real turkey with stuffing and cranberry sauce on a real roll! It always beat the single slice of warm cheese sandwich, or the stinky egg salad on mushy white bread with transparent mayonnaise around the edges. Jillian was beyond grateful when Grandma saved the day. And she always did.

Over the years Jillian got used to looking for Grandma's car at the pick-up line at school whenever her mother forgot. These were happy days because it meant that she didn't have to go home and most likely would be staying at Grandma's for dinner. Sometimes her father would join them after work or before night school. Sometimes they would need to hang out at Grandma's house because the lights went out in their apartment, again. Jillian grew to believe that lights went out in apartments but not in houses; especially not in Grandma's house. That's just how it was.

*

Jillian practically lived at Grandma's house. She found comfort knowing that Grandma could sense her emotions within seconds of seeing her face.

"What's wrong Jillie-Bean?"

Jillian thought about making something up, but it was no use. "Mommy's mad again."

"Why?"

"I don't know." Jillian shrugged. "She just gets mad all the time. She hits me, too."

"I'm so sorry Jillie. I didn't raise her like that. I don't know why she acts that way."

Jillian could hear her grandfather cursing from the yard, beating the daylights out of the ground with a shovel.

"Do you want me to talk to her?"

Jillian froze. She wanted to tell someone, but didn't want to get punished for telling. She knew her secret would be safe with Grandma. "No, Mommy will be madder."

"I'm here for you. If you ever need me, just call me. OK, Jillie-Bean?"

"OK, Grandma."

*

When Jillian was home, she found solace looking out the window of their small apartment. Whenever tears streamed down her face she would study the Birch tree outside. Its silky ebony accents complemented the magic of its chalky complexion. She recalled feeling the contrasting texture between her fingers; the grated coconut-like bark nestled against a smooth ribbon of perfection. She questioned its multiple trunks and had staring contests with the circles she called eyes. The tree watched and protected her. She talked to it every time she had just been beaten for something she may or may not have done. How nice it felt to rest her hot forehead against the cool window for a moment, dreaming. The Birch tree signaled hope of happiness, an escape to a world outside of the courtyard, and something to look forward to every time she was pulled away from the window. She would clamp onto the painted sill with her fingernails, screaming. The Birch tree always understood and waited for her return.

-Chapter Two-

There were no tears the day Jillian moved into her college dorm.

"How independent my little Jillie has become," her mother announced to anyone passing by.

Jillian rolled her eyes when she heard the sentiment for the first time. She walked across the quad and saw parents and kids crying and hugging, saying things like "I'll miss you" and "I love you" and she wondered what that must have felt like.

She wasn't there long when she got her first letter from Grandma, her new pen pal.

"Hi Jillie-Bean, I miss you. Things aren't the same around here now that you aren't here to visit. Well, nothing new here, same old, same old. I hope you're having the time of your life. Well, so long, be good, I love you always, Grandma. PS: Go buy yourself something nice."

Inside was a tightly folded five-dollar bill, enough to buy fried mozzarella at the corner pizza place, a typical Thursday night hang-out.

"Hi Grandma, Thank you for the letter and the money. Things are great here. My roommate is awesome, and I'm learning a lot. I miss you so much. I hope the mailman doesn't forget to bring you this letter. Say Hi to Grandpa. I love you always, Jillie."

As the weeks progressed, Grandma's handwritten letters

became shorter and weirder. Grandpa had had a stroke and passed away and Grandma was all alone.

"Hi Jillie, Nothing new here. Well, I have to go feed the deer and the goats in the yard. They eat right out of my hand. Love, Grandma." Jillian frowned as she put the letter back in the envelope.

When Jillian came home on long-weekends, she couldn't wait to spend time with Grandma. She felt weird in the house without Grandpa but they kept busy playing cards, or Jillian took Grandma shopping. Whenever they went to lunch Jillian had to sneak dollar bills onto the table in addition to the few coins Grandma would always leave as tip. Jillian didn't think anything of it.

- *Chapter Three* -

Jillian enjoyed her independence at college, but that ended after the first semester when the money ran out and she had to move out of the dorms and back home. It didn't take long for her mother to start in on her again.

Something set her off, but what? Jillian was out late with friends the night before and was planning to go out again without permission. Was that it? She had grown accustomed to coming and going and not checking in. She had a job that wasn't until the afternoon, so that wasn't it. She was having fun, was that it?

"You're not going." Jillian's mother was adamant.

"Why?"

"Because I said so."

"That's not a good reason."

Her mother's fist clenched.

Jillian knew the pattern and ran.

Her mother lunged at her, a hot curling iron in her grip. The cord pulled from the outlet, and whipped against the walls in her path. Jillian stumbled to get out of the way. The screaming match and stomping continued up the narrow carpeted staircase. She found herself cornered near the twin bed nearest the window. The flowered bedspreads and frilly matching sham-covered pillows thick, not from stuffing or feathers but from years of heavy tears.

"Mom, stop, don't do this."

"Don't make this about me."

"It's always about you."

"You're such a…"

"Go ahead, what am I?"

"You're a … stupe."

Jillian's mouth curled at the corners. The word "stoop" was her mother's go-to word, intending to reduce Jillian to something below a moron.

Her mother hissed, "I'm gonna brain you."

Jillian started to laugh. "Brain me? Who says that?"

The curling iron came at her head.

Jillian knocked it away. The bedspread sizzled.

Her mother's fist came at her. But this time, instead of cowering, Jillian grabbed her mother's wrist, hard.

"If you hit me, I *will* hit you back." Jillian's eyes narrowed.

Forming some sort of truce, her mother exhaled sharply.

Jillian let go of her mother's wrist and she backed off.

Everything was going great up until that point. The distance was a necessary solution for them. She had been pleased to be able to get along with this woman for the first time; no more slights, no accusations, no fighting. She had expected it to last. She had experienced what it was like to be on her own and saw how loving mothers were *supposed* to treat their kids. She would put a stop to the cycle once and for all. She would move out, but where?

The plan couldn't have been more perfect. Jillian's father helped with what would be her new bedroom at Grandma's house. Fresh paint on walls, tarps on the floor, paintbrushes and a roller in the pan, Billy Joel's "Movin' Out" playing in the background. Jillian and her dad enjoyed a moment to smile at each other without words, just a quick squeeze around the shoulders. She couldn't contain her excitement.

Grandma was excited that she would be around to 'Break up the Monotony' as Grandpa used to say. Jillian got lost in the memories; playing checkers, Rummy, and UNO with him at the kitchen table; a tradition she would continue with Grandma.

-*Chapter Four*-

"I call it my loft." Jillian told her long-time friend and neighbor, Patti, as they bounced toward the staircase in their stretch pants, slouch socks, and patterned sweaters. "I have the whole upstairs; both bedrooms and the bathroom all to myself."

Patti looked around as she walked. "I haven't been in this house since we were kids." She ran her hand along the top of the dresser. "I don't think we were ever allowed up here." She giggled, shrugging her shoulders.

"We weren't, but we did it anyway!"

"Yeah." Patti agreed, "We always snuck back downstairs with bright orange and red lipstick all over our mouths thinking Grandma didn't notice."

"I think about that every time I try to pry open the drawers on this old dresser expecting to see old makeup samples."

Patti smiled. "It looks great up here. Where did all that stuff go that was up here?"

Jillian opened one of the walk-in attic spaces. It was always an adventure to find some kind of missing treasure in there; perfume spritzers with a crusty squeeze pump, old articles about wedding announcements, births, deaths, faux leather pocketbooks, platform shoes, stacks of magazines tied up with yarn.

Patti shuddered at the sight of the styrofoam heads with short curly wigs. "They're still here."

"I know. They always freaked me out, too."

Patti glanced toward the door. "I still feel like we're gonna get in trouble for being up here."

"I know, right?" Jillian looked down at the orange and black carpet remnants covering the floor. "But since Grandma's sciatic nerve hurts her and she's too afraid to walk up the stairs, she won't be running up here with the wooden spoon any time soon."

They laughed.

Between the two attic spaces was a dormer where Jillian had decorated a cozy reading and writing nook. A sectional couch occupied the other half of the room, separating the bedroom and living room areas complete with TV, desk, and artist easel. The "loft" became the perfect studio getaway.

"What the hell is this?" Patti screeched, opening a door with one hand while twirling a piece of her exceptionally curly hair with the other. It wasn't your typical college-girl closet full of shoes and clothes. Yes, there were shoes and clothes. But more than that.

"It's my one-for-you, one-for-me closet, my 'I'm preparing for my own apartment' closet. When I move out," Jillian explained, "I won't have to buy anything."

"You won't have to buy anything into retirement you have so much stuff." Patti smacked her gum. "See this heart trivet?" she pulled the wooden shape out of the closet.

"I love that trivet," Jillian beamed. Patti rolled her eyes, then focused in on the prize. "Hey, you got that for me for my engagement."

"Exactly, one for you, one for me." Jillian snatched it back.

"Brilliant," Patti said before getting lost in her own memory. She stretched her hand out in front of her to find the maximum light reflecting off the crystal clear perfection on her finger. Patti was a few years older and Jillian always looked up to her. She was big the sister she never had. She and her boyfriend had been together since they were kids and Jillian was a little jealous of their 'bestfriendship' and unbreakable love and bond; their true one and only's.

Putting the trivet back in the closet, Jillian scanned the rest of the pile and sighed.

"You ok? Do you like it here Jillie?"

"The house is great ... but Grandma's getting more forgetful by the weeks. I see it more now that I'm here. She knows it, too, and it scares her."

Patti's eyes stared to fill. She'd loved Grandma as if she was her own since she was a little girl hiding on the other side of the forsythia, looking for four-leaf clovers, and putting buttercups under Jillian's chin.

"Poor Grammy. I'm glad you're here with her." She reached for Jillian's arm. "We'd better get back downstairs."

As they made their way down, Grandma shouted, "Jillie, get down here, quick, there's a bear."

Oh boy. "Where?" Jillian yelled.

"In the backyard. In the tree." They made their way first to the window.

"I don't see it."

"Up there," Grandma pointed. "High in the tree. At the tip-py-top."

"It's a raccoon, oh wait, *is* it a bear?"

"What?"

"It's a raccoon," Jillian shouted.

"What?" Grandma's hearing was getting worse.

"It's a raccoon," Jillian shouted louder. Grandma heard her this time.

"It does look like a baby bear. A really big one. He's so cute." Patti added.

"I guess I'll call animal control." Jillian tripped over Patti's foot as she lunged for the phone.

"Umm, I'd better go," Patti hugged her. Tight. "Good luck ... with everything. And again, I'm so glad you're here."

-*Chapter Five*-

Over the next year, aside from some forgetfulness and silly things, living with Grandma was awesome. Jillian gained independence and Grandma had someone checking on her more than usual. They shared stories about life and relationships and secrets and Jillian helped around the house. She was able to take Grandma to doctor's appointments around her school and work schedule. Grandma's sciatic nerve was causing her more pain so it became increasingly difficult to shove her into the car without her crying.

Jillian was able to get a handicap sticker and used it to park right up front. They had to make their way out of the car, up the handicap ramp, into the building, down hallways, up the elevator to the appointment barely on time. "It makes absolutely no sense to have handicapped parking if patients have to hobble across creation to get to the appointment. Seriously." Jillian had not thought to call for a wheelchair; if she had it would have made things much easier. A hearing aid would have helped too but Grandma didn't want one. Jillian recalled the day she drove Grandma home after finally getting her a hearing aid and she was alarmed by hearing a loud swoosh.

"What's that noise?"

"Grandma it's a puddle." Grandma didn't understand.

"We just drove through a puddle. You couldn't hear that before?"

Grandma had a huge smile of wonder on her face. Jillian was excited to share it with her, and not to have to shout anymore.

– Chapter Six –

Jillian was excited for her date. She rushed around the kitchen, making sure Grandma would have water, a snack, and a crossword puzzle before she left.

Grandma watched her run back and forth. "Are you going to a dance?"

"No, Grandma."

"When I was young, we would go to dances."

"No, Grandma, remember? I have a boyfriend now. Hi name is Sean and we're going out to dinner. Do you want to meet him when he shows up?"

Grandma clasped her hands together over her mouth. She didn't remember that Jillian was growing up. In her mind, Jillian was fourteen, maybe even twelve.

"Are you going to wear that?" Grandma tilted her head.

Jillian looked down at her sweater, rolled her eyes, and scrambled up the stairs to find something else to wear. The clock seemed to spit out minutes faster than possible. She threw open the closet door, pulled out a simple dress and heard a car door slam. "Oh God, he's here." She tried to find the opening of the dress to throw on over her head. He was walking up the driveway. "Oh no." She smoothed out the fabric around the waist and flew down the stairs to get to the door first. Too late: Grandma was holding the door open and he was stepping up into the kitchen. They were meeting.

"Grandma this is Sean. Sean this is Grandma."

Grandma didn't say anything but looked up in awe. He was ridiculously handsome, with ethereal blue eyes, and a perfect smile that made Jillian fall in love every time he looked at her. In that moment she watched him with Grandma.

He was over a foot taller than both of them. Grandma eyed him from toe to head, and back down again, her mouth opened. It was like a scene from a movie in slow motion. Jillian knew that whatever she was going to say was not going to be good, so she started shoving Sean back out the door and kissed Grandma on the cheek. "Ok, we're going to be late. Don't stay up." But Grandma was still standing with her mouth open and then she did it. She said something. It was like she couldn't help herself, as if she was yelling 'Fore' from the eighteenth hole. Then, in perfect diction and enunciation, clear as day, she shouted, "HE'S A GIANT."

Jillian froze. Sean threw his head back and laughed.

"I'm SO sorry," Jillian said rushing him away.

"That's ok. I must look like a giant to her. She's cute." Walking down the driveway to the car, Sean shouted 'bye' while Grandma yelled a quick lecture toward the car.

"Never, ever say 'bye'. Say 'so long'. It means I'll see you again."

"Not after this," Jillian mumbled. "Get in."

Grandma proceeded to yell, "Watch the kooks" out the door. But Jillian knew that wasn't it. Sean began walking Jillian to the passenger side, Jillian heard the screen door creak open again. "Oh no." Jillian started shoving Sean to his side of the car.

"What are you doing?"

"You don't have to walk me, get in, *faster.*" Jillian knew what was coming.

Grandma cleared her throat and inhaled. "Keep your legs crossed!" The phrase echoed down the driveway. Sean laughed as he backed out of the driveway and all the way down the street.

Grandma was pacing the kitchen when Sean returned Jillian back home. "Did you take my hearing aid?"

"No, I didn't take it."

"What?"

"No, I didn't take it." Jillian shouted.

 "Did you take my 'choppers'?"

Why the hell would I do that? "No, I didn't take your 'choppers', your teeth? No, now cut it out." Jillian shook her head.

Chapter Seven

The next afternoon, Jillian walked past Grandma sitting by the window. "Grandma, did I get any mail today?"

The answer over the last several months was always the same, "No." She blamed it on the postman, but that wasn't anything new, the family had been hearing that for years. Grandma used to hide the bills from Grandpa so he couldn't get so upset about the "God Damn Money" and the "God Damn Bills" and the "God Damn Conspiracy" and how "even the God Damn tic-tacs got smaller but the prices were getting higher". Jillian recalled Grandpa said "God Damn" a lot which sent her covering her ears and hiding behind the gold corded reading chair in the den when she was little. But a red flag went up regarding Grandma's forgetfulness when Jillian happened to beat Grandma to the mailbox one day on her way home from class.

Jillian took out a handful of late-notices and last call slips. Jillian marched into the house. "I got the mail."

Grandma's eyes opened wide.

"Grandma, have you not been paying the bills?"

"Oh, you know how it is." Grandma pushed past her to change her shoes. "I suppose I don't need these if you already got the mail."

A feeling gripped Jillian's heart when she realized that one of the few things left that Grandma looked forward to every day was walking to the end of the driveway to get the mail and that was taken away. She didn't know what to say. She held back her tears.

Grandma shuffled back, her feet comforted in pink day slippers. She reached into her sleeve for her tissue and flopped backward into the octagonal upholstered throne. "Ugh," she grunted as she landed. She was swallowed up instantly in the gaudy pattern of the chair; bright red and orange flowers, outlined in thick black lines. She reached a long filed fingernail out to snap the wide metal venetian blinds open.

"That darned mailman doesn't know how to deliver the mail to the right address. I've been waiting for him all day, when is he going to come?"

Jillian opened her mouth and inhaled sharply, but no words came out. She couldn't think of a response.

Grandma looked toward the two massive evergreens that stood at attention at each side of the mailbox; the mailbox that her grandfather had rigged years ago so the neighborhood boys couldn't knock it down with bats as they sped by. The mailbox that was empty.

Jillian looked out too. Maybe the mailman forgot something and would have to come back. There was no sign of him anywhere. She scanned the front yard past the boxwood hedges that lined the front of the yard and past the enormous snowball bushes, as large as trees, that marked the side yard property line. Jillian remembered a huge battle between her grandfather and the neighbor who liked to creep up as close as possible to the invisible property line, but her grandfather knew the survey plans and wouldn't give a quarter of an inch. She recalled the dried snowball bouquets blowing around like tumbleweed on windy days. Her gaze came back around to the magnolia tree which bloomed in front of the large picture window where Grandma liked to sit and observe. It had one horizontal branch protruding from the trunk about three feet off the ground that all the kids loved to hang from or climb up and sit on. It wasn't sturdy, but bouncy and that made it fun. Even the neighbor's grandkids enjoyed sitting in the tree when they were in town. Everyone loved to pluck the leathery leaves and rub the velvety softness on their faces or pretend to be various animals because the leaves looked and felt like furry ears. Inevitably, the kids were always shooed out of the tree and left to mope. No one understood why they weren't allowed to play in the tree.

On the other side of the driveway, two not-so-fabulous Crab apple trees did nothing but shed tiny worm-ridden fruit that everyone had to pitch in to help rake into smelly piles and pick up. All the cousins learned the value of hard work in the form of blisters throughout multiple seasons. Whether it was apples, lilacs, berries, or leaves, they were put to work raking piles. Science experiments ensued while the kids pet, taunted, or even impaled furry gypsy caterpillars just to prove what color their blood was. Countless unsuspecting butterfly beauties were captured just long enough to examine the curve of their antennae, the detail of their wings, their eyes, their mouths, their prickly feet, yet long enough for the butterfly to sit for a while before realizing it was free to fly away.

The venetian blind cracked shut.

Jillian started to watch Grandma's every move over the next few days. She spied while Grandma went to the mailbox, and especially when she rummaged around in the top drawer of her dresser. Jillian became increasingly suspicious of what she was doing in there.

"Tomorrow," Jillian said to herself, "When Grandma's distracted, I'm going to find out what's in that damn drawer."

-Chapter Eight-

"Grandma, I'm home." Groceries, keys, purse, dumped upon entry.

"Hi," Grandma said pleasantly but cautiously; a cup of tea in hand, syrupy sweet.

"What's wrong?"

Grandma looked confused. "You stole my teeth."

"Um, no, I didn't steal your teeth."

"You did."

"We're not having this conversation. *Again.* I didn't take your teeth. I didn't take your hearing aid."

"I need to eat more fish."

"You want fish?"

"For brain food."

"Oh. Well, I just went to the store, but I didn't buy fish."

"Do you want …" Grandma searched for the word. "Do you want crayons for lunch?" Grandma asked.

Jillian tried to overlook the mistake. "I bought lunchmeat and rolls. I'd rather have that."

Grandma paused and sighed. Any expression drained from her face. "I can't remember the words. The golden years. They're not so golden ... they're a little bit rusty."

Jillian sat down at the table. "It's ok, I'm here to help." She took Grandma's hands in her own, feeling her ivory-smooth skin.

Grandma shook her head. "I'm losing my mind and there's nothing I can do about it." Her voice broke as soon as the words were uttered. Jillian watched her eyes fill.

Grandma shook it off, tapped her temple and blurted out, "BING ... pick up the marbles." They both giggled.

"Everyone gets a little forgetful sometimes. I'm making sandwiches for lunch. We're going to have lunch and then I have to go to class. What are you doing today, cracking the code on the lottery numbers?"

"No." Grandma wasn't interested in the numbers. It had been a few weeks since she took a notebook and pen out to analyze her lists, statistics, and charts of probabilities as to which numbers would be most likely to emerge in the cage of balls as the winners. "Are you going to watch your 'story'?" Jillian was surprised she wasn't waiting for it to come on, nearly missing her one-hour time slot. They both looked up at the clock without saying anything. Jillian set up a sandwich and tea on the tray table in front of Grandma's chair, positioned for easy television viewing and directly in front of the big window so she wouldn't miss anything.

"There's less hopping in and out of bed on this show," Grandma remembered proudly.

"Right," Jillian agreed. It was a justification Jillian heard every single weekday for as long as she could remember.

"Also…"

Jillian knew what she was going to say.

"They show less titties on this story." Yup, she went there. The 'titties' line. It was Jillian's favorite Grandma-ism and always a conversation stopper.

"Um, Grandma, that word doesn't mean what you *think* it means … anymore."

"What word?"

"*That* word," Jillian couldn't bring herself to say it. "People don't use that word to describe a man's bare chest anymore." It was a repeat conversation that Jillian couldn't endure again.

It was unlike Grandma to miss her "story" or not be busy doing something. Often, she could be found knitting or sitting at the kitchen table exercising her "brain muscles" with crossword puzzles from the daily newspaper, or playing Solitaire. She would always lecture anyone who would listen about the importance of reading to keep the brain active and healthy. She would endlessly try to figure out the pattern for the winning Lotto numbers, exacting her formula's for picking the right numbers this time. She had countless piles of black composition notebooks filled to the brim with list of numbers in carefully ruled columns. Running to the convenience store with her pre-filled-out-sheets of the numbers that came to her in her dream the night before was a common occurrence or looking up her dreams in the dream book if she could remember them. She couldn't be bothered with people her age. She would refer to them as "old people complaining about their aches and pains and wasting time with petty gossip", so the senior center was never for her. She loved being home.

When a new commercial came on, Grandma repeated, "There's less hopping in and out of bed on this show."

"Yes." Jillian wondered if Grandma was excited to be able to say it or whether she didn't remember she just said it.

Jillian strained to hear if the mail truck was coming over the thundering console television. "Grandma, the mailman's coming down the road."

"No, I just went out. We didn't get anything."

Jillian nodded slowly. Her detective work would have to wait until the next day.

Jillian had occupied herself upstairs with other things when she heard the screen door creak open downstairs. She paused and tilted her head like a dog hearing the treat box being opened across the house. She shot from zero to a sprint, down five stairs at a time. Her heart pounded in her throat. She peeked outside to see a displaced New England winter Grandma decked out in full coat, hat, gloves, purple sweat pants and brown dress loafers making her way down the sweltering summer landscape. *Oh God, she's gonna freakin' boil.* Jillian didn't have time to pick this battle. It was time for the undercover mission. She knew that she had no more than a few minutes. She tingled with anticipation, adrenaline pumping, spy-themed music pounding in her temples.

Jillian opened the top dresser drawer and heard a piercing squeal. The hearing aid. She moved a stack of nightgowns around to look for it, but carefully so Grandma wouldn't notice anything out of place. She found the hearing aid and all of Grandma's treasures; a bag full of ceramic figurines from the Red Rose tea bag collection, an elf figurine with a fuzzy pom-pom at the end of his hat, and curled up postage stamps that she had steamed off of envelopes at some point. Next to that lived some old wheat pennies, a yellowed plastic daisy magnet, and a mint green container with a lid. Her 'choppers'. Jillian winced.

Moving on to the underwear pile, she uncovered checks, checkbooks, check registries, savings books, bounced checks, overdue bills and pink-enveloped cancellation notices. "Bingo." She took out only what was necessary to make phone calls about and returned the treasures to their original spots.

She turned the volume down on the hearing aid, wiped the wax off with a tissue, trying not to gag. She ran to put the container of teeth in the bathroom vanity, the place they had lived for a quarter of a century, threw a pile of bills upstairs, and came back down to put the hearing aid on the table with only a second to spare before Grandma returned.

"Whoo, it's hot out there," Grandma exclaimed when she came back inside. Jillian helped her remove her hat and coat. Her hair was sweat-plastered to her forehead.

"Here." Jillian helped Grandma get settled in at the table with a crossword puzzle and a glass of water. "Ok, I'm getting ready to leave for class."

"What?" Grandma shouted.

Jillian pointed to the hearing aid and Grandma took it and put it in her ear without question.

"Do you need anything? You have water, newspaper, glasses, crossword puzzle, pencil."

"Nope, I'm just waiting for the mailman. That darned mailman doesn't know how to deliver the mail to the right address. I've been waiting for him all day, when is he going to come?"

Jillian stopped short and looked through the window to the backyard for an answer. "Umm, Grandma, you just got the mail."

"If you say so."

"I say so. It's right here on the table." Jillian thumbed through it quickly to know what to look for later in the drawer. "Look, I have to go to class. Don't go outside. Don't let anyone in the house. Don't sign anything. Don't buy anything. Do not let ANY-ONE into the house. So long, love you, I'll be back soon. My schedule's on the fridge."

"See you soon, Jillie-Bean."

At least she knows who I am.

*

Jillian tried to concentrate while the professor droned on.

"The Birch tree symbolizes change."

Jillian froze.

"People used to write poetry and emotional messages on Birch bark."

She remembered the Birch tree outside her apartment window, the tears, being pulled away from the window. She thought about the large pine trees at the end of Grandma's driveway, the mail, Grandma waiting for the mailman. What if Grandma goes outside in her coat and hat again. What if she falls and no one is there to help?

Jillian clutched her stomach. Pains began to form. She pushed the chair away from the desk, ran out of class, through the quad, and past the statue that represented her school, to her car.

Jillian was careful to slow down before entering Grandma's driveway. *OK, she's not in the driveway. Good. No flames in the windows. Door's closed. Check. Nothing blaringly weird. Good. No screaming.* Her visions of being the one to find her on the floor absolutely terrified her, every time.

Stop it. I can't live my life thinking this way and being afraid. Enjoy the good times. She loves having me here. Enjoy it. Stop being so afraid all the time, it's not healthy. OK, deep breath. Go in, it's fine.

Jillian peeked in the window on the door. The frilly curtains didn't cover the sides and she found that she could see in. First she looked toward the living room, she wasn't there. Then she looked toward the kitchen table. Then she saw Grandma's white head resting face-down on the table. *Oh my God.* Jillian fumbled to get the door unlocked. She swung the door open so forcefully it hit the wall. Jillian lunged toward the table.

Grandma popped her head up, startling them both.

"What's wrong?"

"You didn't tell me you were going to be gone."

"Grandma, I go to school every day."

"If you say so."

Jillian could feel her jaw clench. "I left the schedule on the fridge. Did you remember I left it on the fridge for you?"

"Yes." Grandma twisted the ring on her left finger.

"So why didn't you look at it?" Jillian snapped, snatching the paper. "I wrote out my entire schedule for you hour-by-hour so you wouldn't make yourself sick worrying about me. Today's Wednesday," Jillian pointed. "On Wednesday's I come home at three o'clock, but I'm early today." She looked at Grandma's face which was knitted in confusion, intently trying to solve the complex algorithm, looking up with a blank stare.

Jillian took a step back. "Oh my God," she whispered. *She can't figure out the day and time.*

"I can't remember ... I forgot to ... " She tapped the side of her head with her finger. "Bing!"

Jillian tilted her head in empathy. Grandma bit her lip, not knowing what to say. Tears formed in both their eyes as they studied each other.

"How did this happen to me?"

"Awww Grandma, I'm here now, what did you need?"

Grandma shook her head.

"I want to help you. That's why I'm here."

"I was just writing a check but I couldn't remember —"

"I'll do it."

Grandma smashed her hand on the table. "I'm perfectly capable of handling the bills and the finances."

"Ok." Jillian decided to trust her. Grandma would just write a check and everything would be fine.

*

Sean's house was Jillian's welcomed retreat and his couch was a place to recuperate in his arms while he watched sports. Most times she fell asleep while he rubbed her back or her feet. This time, she needed to talk about Grandma and her forgetfulness. He tried to comfort her as best he knew, but she couldn't stay calm. She was worried about leaving Grandma alone.

When she returned from Sean's early, she saw Grandma sitting at the kitchen table again, a pile of bills, a calculator and checkbook in front of her. Her head rested in her hands like she had a headache or was crying. "Grandma, what's wrong?"

"I just don't understand." Grandma said. "It's simple addition and subtraction, yet I just can't seem to get it right."

"I told you I will help you figure it out."

Grandma squinted. "I've been balancing my checkbook since before you were born. I'm very good at math. I've always kept my checking account in good working order. I. Don't. NEED. YOUR. Help."

Jillian was taken aback. Grandma had not spoken to her that way since she was seven years old after the cousins were in a debate about who would touch the iron to see how hot it *really* was. Inevitably over the course of a decade each child ended up crying, holding up a pulsing, scorched, butter-glistened finger. In that moment, Jillian became seven again, ashamed for disappointing her beloved grandmother while her grandfather tossed expletives in the background.

"Grandma, it's not that I doubt your ability, it's just that since I live here now, you should relax. Let me take care of the bills so you don't have to. That's why I'm here."

When Grandpa passed, Grandma had found her independence. She took her time at the store or running errands. She knitted and crocheted, always had a cup of syrupy-sweet tea in her hand. She loved watching her "story" at 2pm, the one with Tina, and Vicki who turned into Niki who then turned back into Vicki. When Jillian was younger, she always tried to cake on the lip gloss the way Tina did and couldn't help wonder if Larry was a doctor, why didn't he remove the mole on his face himself.

But Grandma wasn't doing those things anymore. It was rare that she was interested in watching her "story" anymore. Instead, she started doing odd things. On this particular day, she proudly announced that she would just close her checking account and would be driving to each of the billing locations to pay the bills with cash.

"Do you even know where the water company is?"

"Yes, it's over by the Fairway Beef."

"Grandma, the water company has never even been in this town and Fairway Beef isn't there anymore, it closed. Actually, it burned down."

Grandma gasped. She didn't remember. It had been over a decade since Grandpa was a butcher there and all the kids used to visit him in the walk-in meat locker, freezing their tiny flip-flopped feet off. As they got older, they found it embarrassing to be acknowledged by the man in the white paper hat and blood-stained apron in the big freezer. But Fairway Beef was a staple in the community. It was the place to go for fresh quality meat and everyone in town knew that because the storefront window was in the shape of a cow.

"Grandma, you cannot pay these bills in person. It doesn't work like that anymore. The billing address for this one is ... five states away."

"Oh," listening but not fully processing.

"Don't worry," Jillian assured her, "I'll help you, don't worry. Do not close the account." Grandma seemed to understand and Jillian was relieved.

-Chapter Nine-

The next day was an early class schedule and Jillian was home in plenty of time to join Grandma in her sunny kitchen. "Come here. Let me do your nails," Grandma said, thrilled. Spaced out evenly on the table were nail clippers, files, cuticle cutters, polish, and remover. Jillian was shocked by her clarity and ability. It was salon time!

"Put your hands on the table and don't move." Jillian became a child again in that moment. She had sat at Grandma's kitchen table nail salon since before she was barely old enough to see over the sparkly formica without a booster. Three strokes. Right side, left side, and one quick swoop down the middle. Right side, left side, middle. Don't dawdle or go over it too many times while it's wet. If you mess up, fix it later. A ritual she would recall far into adulthood.

"So tell me, are you sweet on anyone?" Grandma pried. She held Jillian's hand and looked at her face.

She doesn't remember.

Jillian looked down at Grandma's hands. They always looked so young and smooth. Jillian loved staring at the simple channel cut diamond ring on Grandma's left finger and wondered if one day she would ever share it with her as her wedding band.

"That's okay, you're young. Don't rush into wanting to be married. I never wanted to be married you know." Grandma confided.

"What?" Jillian's mouth dropped. "I knew Grandpa had a pretty rough temper, especially in the garden, but ... "

"Your grandfather pursued me so hard. I was, as far as he knew, single."

"So that was it? Didn't you love him? Didn't you want someone there by your side, have children?"

"No, I was going to be a bachelorette, but back then it was looked down upon. I was in my thirties and already considered an Old Maid, a Spinster."

Jillian shrugged her shoulders. "Didn't you want to be in love?"

"I was in love once. Before I met your grandfather," Grandma continued. It wasn't what Jillian expected. She always thought Grandma ended up marrying her grandfather because the 'pickin's were slim'. This was a new and exciting change of events.

"We were engaged. He died in the war," Grandma's eyes went to a place very far away.

"I didn't know that," whispered Jillian.

"No one did." Grandma tightened the cap on the nail polish. The pair sat in silence. Jillian waited for more. "We sent letters back and forth, until one day a package with different handwriting showed up from the same address. I couldn't breathe. I just knew. I still remember his words.

"My dearest Heloise,

If you are reading this, it is because something bad has happened and I had given instruction for this letter to be sent to you. You are the love of my life. My one and only love. Your smile and sense of humor warm me to my core and whenever I am scared or lonely, I press your letters to my chest knowing you are the one thing I have to live for. You know you are the first thing I think of when I wake, the last thing before I retire, and the only thing I dream about when I get out of here. You are my everything and I can't wait to make you my bride.

But something has happened. Something awful darlin', if you are reading this. I want you to promise me you will marry, have a family, give it a chance. You have no reason to put that on hold. I

don't want you to be alone. I know this will not change your feelings for me. I'll see you soon, on the other side.
　Love Forever,
　Jackie."

Jillian stayed silent.
"I found out he died that night."
"I'm so sorry Grandma, I had no idea."
"I know." She returned the cuticle cutters to their leather pouch.
"Bachelorette, huh?"
Grandma shrugged her shoulders. "Things don't always happen the way you've planned."
Jillian thought about how Grandma must have felt on the day of his funeral. She imagined the smoothness of the casket, the crisp folds of the American flag, the medals of honor, the flowers, the lilies, the powdery golden-yellow pollen on the anthers and the silky meatiness of the petals. "Is that why you hate lilies?"
"No, but how on earth would you remember that?"
Jillian shrugged.
"When my mother died, they had lilies all around her. And they picked me up and leaned me into the casket. She had lots of makeup on and dark red lipstick. She never wore dark red lipstick. She wore bright red lipstick. Her brows were drawn on, but not quite right. They held me over her for a long time and they waited until I kissed her. They made me kiss her. She was so still and so cold. I hate open caskets. I hate lilies."
"Grandma, it's just a flower." Jillian bit her lip as soon as she said it. "You want me to help you with the checkbook?
"I closed the account."
"You what?"
"I ... don't be upset with me."
"I'm not upset, get dressed, we're going to the bank."
Jillian waited an eternity for Grandma to get dressed. Her bare feet cradled in brown slip-on loafers with fringe-cut faux leather accents, brown slacks, a brown striped top complete with large bow, her hand-crocheted pink sweater over that. She combed her

hair, and put her 'choppers' and hearing aid in.

Jillian remembered opening the door to that same bank with Grandma when she was about six to open a savings account. It was back when the account holders held savings books, before ATMs, and when the banks gave away cool stuff like Jillian's prairie girl piggy bank. It was delicate ceramic, all white except for the girl's eyes and lips. She wore a bonnet, and a dress with a petticoat that had a pocket in the front where a tiny dog lived. It didn't take long for a long crack to form along the back of the bonnet at the coin slot from being clunked around too much and for the dog to wander away. Jillian LOVED that piggybank with every bit of her being. She smiled at the memory.

"I can help you over here." Grandma shuffled to the first small cubicle office on the corner to make the transaction official. A lot of paperwork was exchanged back and forth. Grandma had a confused look on her face. "You know Heloise, it's great that you have such a wonderful granddaughter to help you." Grandma didn't respond, but her face lit up and she reached out to tap Jillian's hand. A slight smile invaded the corners of Jillian's lips. Her mind tug-o-warred the past and the present realities. *Today was a good day.*

-Chapter Ten-

Grandma became more forgetful as the months passed. One night, when Jillian and Sean were hanging out in the loft, they heard banging and screaming in the other room. Jillian ran through the living room to the kitchen where she found her grandmother beating the crap out of the brand new black glass-top stove with a ceramic spoon rest. Her arm was up and she was about to smash it down again when Jillian grabbed hold of it.

"What are you doing? You're gonna break it," Jillian screeched.

"I hate this stove, it's black."

"And the problem is?"

"What are we, slaves?"

Jillian froze, Sean was within earshot. Jillian had never heard her grandmother speak like this before. She had no idea Grandma felt this way.

"Shhhhh ... What? That makes no sense." Jillian shrugged her shoulders.

"I want my old stove back," Grandma whimpered. She raised the spoon rest to smash it down on the glass-top again. Jillian grabbed it back. She looked at the new stove and saw how mismatched it looked against the old avocado "ice box". The new replaced the old, but carelessly intruded on what used to be familiar.

"Grandma, it didn't work so we got you this new one." Jillian tried to reassure her.

"I. Don't. Like. It."

"This is what we have now. I can't do anything about it." It was clear that neither of them would win this argument.

Jillian backed up, reached for the newspaper, fluffed out a few pages, found the crossword puzzle and put it on the table. She checked to see if the nubby point on the green number two pencil would suffice. Grandma was immediately distracted.

Flustered and embarrassed, Jillian skulked into the room, wondering how much Sean had heard.

She peeked into the doorway about to apologize.

"Why don't you just move out," he blurted.

Jillian stopped, sucked in her lip deciding how to respond. Barely audible, she whispered, "I could never leave her." Her eyes welled-up, partly for everything that was happening, but mostly for the fact that after all this time, Sean didn't understand. She struggled to get the words out. "You don't just throw someone away because they're sick. I won't leave her as long as she still knows who I am, as long as she still recognizes me. How long will that be? I have no idea." Jillian held back the explosion of tears until Sean left.

*

Over the next several months, the routine and conversations were the same day in and day out. *Grandma I'm home, Grandma I'm going to school, Grandma I'm Jillian, Grandma I'm home, Don't you have to go to class? Grandma it's Sunday. Don't you have to go to school today? If you say so.*

Every day Jillian would get Grandma fed and settled for the day. Then she would go to class and rush back to her second round of classes, and scurry home to feed Grandma dinner, and get her settled for the night. Everything was scheduled around Grandma and high adrenaline.

On this particular day, Grandma was napping when Jillian got home. Jillian sat in the quiet comfort of the loft; silence surrounded her like a bubble. She called Patti to chat.

- Chapter Eleven -

"Hey girl, how's everything going? How's that gorgeous boy-friend of yours?"

"Oh, fine," she lied. Patti knew and waited. "Sean's fine, I don't get to see him a lot because I'm busy with Grandma and class but ... Grandma's getting really forgetful."

"Yeah, she told me about a pig or a goat coming into the garden with her. I had no idea what she was talking about. What is she talking about Jills? Is she ok?"

"That's up for debate I guess," Jillian admitted. "She told me she was in the garden and two deer, not a goat, came into the fenced-in area with her and how she pet them and fed them vegetables. But, would two deer, or any wild animal for that matter, actually walk into a ten-by-ten foot fenced in area with a person?"

"Are you saying it didn't really happen?"

"I'm saying it's up for debate. And she's been saying that people have been walking around the house all dressed up in suits. Just today she worried herself into a tizzy because someone came in the house and ran upstairs. I always tell her not to let anyone in the house and not to sign anything. The last thing we need is for her to sign the house away not knowing what she was doing ... Hello?" Silence filled the other end of the line for a moment.

"Jills, that was me. I was there today. I wasn't in a suit or a dress, but that was me."

Jillian paused, trying to process this.

"I stopped by quick, it wasn't planned so I didn't call you. And

I didn't go upstairs. We sat in the kitchen and she told me about the goat. She knew who I was. She had to."

"I'm nervous. She's getting so forgetful."

"What about driving?"

"No, I think she's fine there. She's traveled these roads for more than half her life. She knows where she is, that's not a problem. I'm more concerned about other people when 'Mario' is out on the road."

"Andretti might be safe, but when Grandma rolls through stop signs in that blazing Skylark, everyone better stay off the sidewalk, curbs, and front yards."

"Haha, well it's not like we can't see that bright orange tank coming from a mile away anyway."

They laughed.

"Um, Patti, I have to go. Grandma's doing something downstairs."

"I thought she was in bed."

"So did I."

Jillian made her way down the stairs and Grandma was sitting at the kitchen table. Jillian leaned toward her for a closer view. What are you eating?"

"Ham."

"How did you cook that?" The stove was unplugged so she wouldn't accidentally leave it on and burn the house down.

"I cooked it," Grandma said proudly.

"How?"

"In the oven."

"You can't eat that, it's not cooked."

"Yes I can. The salt is a preservative."

Jillian inspected the gelatinous chunk of flesh in the fishnet package on the table. It was enough to make her reject all meat completely. Jillian reached for the nearest phone, Grandma's landline, and impatiently twirled the numbers on the old rotary for the poison control number that was taped onto the side of the tan box. *Get her a push button phone.*

"Hello, um, my grandmother is chowing down on a chunk of raw ham from the fridge," Jillian blurted out.

"Ok, stay calm," the representative sing-sang into the phone trying to reassure her. "Most of the time those are cooked already. Can you check the packagin' precious?" She pictured a big-haired diner waitress snapping her gum.

Jillian stretched the cord as far as it would go. "Hold on, cord ... won't ... reach," she grunted and propped the receiver up on the back of the chair against the wall and ran for the cold, crinkly packaging. Jillian read it to the lady on the phone. "Yes, it says pre-cooked. Oh thank God!"

"Great, you're fine then precious!" The conversation ended with pleasantries.

Why the heck all the fuss about bringing the meat to a certain internal temperature if it's cooked already?

Jillian quickly heated up left-over Chinese food (not ham) for Grandma and waited for her to finish eating. It didn't take long because Grandma had already filled up on the ham.

Jillian waited for Grandma and her walker to clink through the house and plop down in front of the television. Outside, the neighborhood was eerily quiet and a thick fog filled the air around her.

It was a quiet day until bedtime.

-Chapter Twelve-

Jillian helped Grandma into bed for the evening and it wasn't long before she dozed off, too. The stress was getting the best of her and she was happy to put the day behind them.

Hours later, Jillian heard a creak and a bang. She sat up, inhaled, and froze. The only things that moved were her eyes. *Is that the screen door? Crash. Bang. Oh my God, someone's opening the door. Someone is here.* The latch on the metal frame clicked into place. It was too deliberate for the wind to be catching it, a hand was forcing it. The door creaked open again, and slammed shut. *Oh my God.* Jillian's imagination ran down the stairs to confront the ax-murderer-killer or was it a gun that he would have ready when she neared the door? She played out the scenario as if she was writing a screenplay. *Hurry, hurry, hurry. Go downstairs. I can't. You have to. What if he hurts Grandma.* She headed for stairs, but stopped. *He can't get you up here.* Then Jillian heard Grandma's voice shout out something she couldn't understand. *Grand ... ma...*

"You can come in".

What the? No, no, no, don't let anyone in. Jillian ran down the stairs. Her heart pounded in her throat with every step. A cool, damp breeze, and the smell of rain hit her though she wasn't able to process what was happening. Grandma stood in the doorway, her white nightgown, flowed and flapped from the gust coming in the door. Grandma opened and slammed the door as if to get someone's attention. Her nostrils flared.

Jillian took a deep breath and shoved Grandma aside to face the crazed lunatic. She pushed her way past Grandma nearly knocking her over, but no one was at the door. She inhaled and leaned her head around the corner. No one was there. Jillian slammed the door shut and locked it.

Grandma stood and stared. Her pupils were enlarged like saucers. Her eyes, translucent and gray. Her skin, a ghostly white. A chill shot through Jillian's body. Grandma stared through her, looking possessed.

"Grandma, are you ok? What are you doing?"

"I'm telling the people in the car that they can come in."

Jillian's face paled like she herself had seen a ghost.

"No one's in the car. That's my car and it's locked."

"I see them".

"Who?"

"Them."

"Who them?

"Them them."

"OK now you're scaring me. I don't know what you're talking about," Jillian pleaded." There's no one there."

"In the car." Grandma pointed a frail, wrinkled finger toward the driveway. They both looked through the window.

"Grandma, that's my car, there's no one in it."

"I see them. Right there in the light."

Another chill went up Jillian's spine.

Grandma stuck to her conviction. Jillian unlocked the door and they looked out again. "That's the reflection of the light on the windshield."

Grandma began to let out a long, ear-piercing scream, not unlike that of a toddler.

"What are you doing? Stop that. Be quiet."

It took another hour to get her back in bed.

Jillian opened the door again to take one more look outside before going to lie in her bed, her mind racing.

What if there were spirits in the car that only Grandma could see? Well, I don't want them in the house. She shuddered. Would the spirits need permission or need to be invited in or would they just show up? She drifted back to sleep.

- Chapter Thirteen -

"She looked right through me, doctor, like she was sleepwalking. It was like an out of body experience. And she got upset like a toddler having a tantrum. There was absolutely no rationalizing or justifying."

Doctor D. went out into the hall to get the nurse and bring in the E.K.G. machine and some other things.

Grandma studied the painting on the wall, curiously. It was an antique painting of a stern-faced woman dressed in frills stiffly buttoned up to her neck. She was adorned with strands of yellow gold and beads of creamy pearls. An extravagant hat of lace and trinkets filled her room. She sat properly upright with gloved hands in her lap. She was neither happy nor sad. Jillian and Grandma both jumped when the door flew open and Doctor D. walked in front of the painting and sat down, redirecting them. He started with a list of questions. "Heloise, can you tell me what year it is?"

"1988, no," she thought for a moment, "1998". Doctor D. wrote it down.

"Who is the President of the United States? What am I holding in my hand? Who am I? Who is with you today? What is your name? What is the day today? Can you look at the clock and tell me the time?"

"Heck, I hardly know what date it is," Jillian commented quietly.

"SLOW but accurate, she's still got it, mostly. I wouldn't diagnose this as Alzheimer's ... yet. Forgetfulness, mild dementia symptoms. Yes. And. You. Little Miss," he tapped Grandma on her shoulder, "have a heart as healthy as a horse."

Grandma smiled.

"There could have been a possible trigger from the Chinese food. Do you know if there was MSG?"

Jillian shrugged her shoulders. She felt responsible. *This could have been avoided? Not Alzheimer's ... yet?* Jillian hung onto the smallest largest word in that sentence, 'yet'. *So, did the chicken and broccoli, and pork fried rice cause the hallucinations? Was it the salt in the ham? This has now jumped rather abruptly up the charts to something horrific, harsh, and real. What is happening?*

"What you witnessed was Sundowning." Doctor D. continued. "Usually this type of thing happens in the early evening, when the sun sets, they just can't adjust to the change." Doctor D. was speaking directly to Jillian. "I think she's been hiding a lot of this for a long time, worse than we thought. At this point I think we can fully diagnose this is a type of dementia, but I'm not sure if this is Alzheimer's." He lowered his voice, "I would, however, think about the car, sooner than later." Grandma didn't hear or at least acknowledge it.

Jillian and Grandma thanked the doctor and the nurses as they left the office complex. *It's not Alzheimer's ... but it's something.*

*

Back home safely, Jillian was upstairs when the phone blasted loud enough downstairs for the neighbors to want to come over and answer it. Grandma must have been walking by because it didn't take her long to lift it from the cradle. Jillian knew it was her mother but she couldn't hear the conversation. Seconds later, it was no surprise when her mother called her phone upstairs.

"Hi."

Her mother was hesitant. "I just talked to Grandma."

"I was just about to call you," Jillian lied. "What did she tell you?"

"She said you took her on a bus," she blurted out, "and there was a big function, but it was in your yard and everyone was dressed up in fancy hats and there were a bunch of folding chairs."

Jillian gave her mother a second to breathe. "Mom, you know I took her to Doctor D. today. You were supposed to meet us there. She rode in the front seat of my car. There were white wooden chairs in the waiting room and antique paintings on the walls." Jillian waited. "Mom." She broke the silence. "It's as we suspected and we have to figure out what to do with the car –"

"That car is her source of freedom and independence," her mother interupted. "She won't understand. She doesn't go far, she knows where she is. She's not ready for that yet. Taking that away from her will kill her."

-*Chapter Fourteen*-

It was a perfectly cheery day on Sterner Road a few weeks later. The dementia diagnosis existed, but daily life continued. Warm sunlight poured into Grandma's brightly painted kitchen. Canary yellow walls and matching painted metal cabinets beamed beneath the mint green leaves that she had stenciled herself so proudly so many decades ago. The soothing rays bounced off the ridged-chrome table and flooded the geometric pattern in the linoleum floor tiles. The sunbeams melted into the avocado fridge with the "ice box" at the bottom. It held ice cream, meats and frosty ice cube trays with a handle that crunched when the lever was lifted. Careful not to pinch fingers or get skin stuck on the metal because of the subzero temps. The glass top stove became a non-issue.

"How do you feel today Grandma?"

Without missing a beat, Grandma revealed a toothless, mischievous grin and tapped her nails on the formica tabletop. "With my hands!"

Jillian couldn't hide her expression. "That's so cute. You're playing a joke on me!" She knew that 'today would be a good day' so she planned to stop at the store on the way home and wouldn't feel badly about it.

Class went by pretty quickly and Jillian remembered at the last second that she had to go to the store for Grandma. She took a right turn on Stillson instead of turning left at the three-way stop onto Woodridge, the infamous hill. It was the hill all the neighborhood friends skinned their knees on while rushing down toward

Tahmore Drive with pails and towels and flip-flopped feet on their way to swim at Lake Mohegan. It was the hill where her friend lived and where they learned to make tissue paper flowers with pipe cleaner stems that looked as real as any kid could imagine. It was the hill that they never wanted to walk back up. She looked around remembering laughter and carefree days at Grandma's house. She passed the handmade signs of the little house on the corner selling tomatoes and fresh eggs. She wondered if the cow still grazed there.

On the way, she remembered what used to be just up ahead on Black Rock Turnpike, Miro Farms. There, they bought whatever vegetables Grandpa didn't have luck growing in his garden that year. Fish at Swanson's was bought when Grandpa didn't wrangle enough fish out of Long Island Sound on his own. Jillian remembered the kitchen table being lined with newspaper and large bluefish. She remembered the bluefish having a strong taste and Grandpa saying, "Fish should never smell fishy."

He always had a fit if Grandma served him chicken even though he brought it home from his butcher shop. It was ok for everyone else to eat chicken, but he said they were "dirty birds that ate their own poop" so he would never eat it. But Grandma made wonderful meals with chicken thighs, chicken breast, chicken pieces, and chicken in cream of celery soup with creamy potatoes. Jillian's mouth watered thinking about the meals that Grandma had forgotten how to make and she wished she had asked for her to write them down. Scups, Hungarian desserts, wrapped cookie kiffles with lekvar or apricot filling. Cheese blintzes or oatmeal cookies.

Fresh. Everything was fresh. Meat was brought home as soon as Grandpa cut it in the shop. Grandma had a grinder to grind meat for homemade sausage and stuffed cabbage. *You always have to know what is in your sausage.* It was a pretty good mantra in Jillian's opinion. The kids were used to knowing where their meals came from and gutting and boning fish or meat was just part of the process. Jillian's stomach growled.

As Jillian sat in a back-up of traffic, she reminisced about going down this road in over 100 degree weather in the white

Fairlane that Grandma called "Betsey". The Fairlane was Grandma's car. She didn't drive the Skylark until Grandpa got sick and couldn't drive anymore. Squished in with all the cousins in their bathing suits and smacking each other with pails, they made their way down Stillson, past Fairfield University and the all-boys high school Fairfield Prep, across the Post Road to get to Jennings beach. Sometimes for a treat, they could go to Penfield beach depending on the tide since they could walk out pretty far at low tide. That sand bar was the softest on their feet.

A kid on a lap in the front passenger seat with Auntie and the other kids sitting on each other's sweaty laps in the back bench seat was the way everyone traveled to the beach. Grandma was the resident and had the free admission sticker. They gulped down even amounts of gas tank and exhaust fumes, but that's how it was, a necessity if they wanted to get to the beach. They enjoyed singing loudly, and pressing fish faces against the tiny obtuse side windows. Inevitably someone would always turn upside-down and think it was funny to foot-wave at the cars behind them.

Seatbelts were the burning hot things that were stuck deep under the seats and if they were able to find them they'd be too cruddy to use, making the finder's hand sludgy with brown/black gunk, so it was deemed 'not worth the trouble, it's only a five-minute ride'. Jillian smiled at the memories. She still remembered the shape and design of the metal on the steering wheel, the smell of the interior, the sound of the engine, and the red ribbon that Grandma superstitiously believed was good luck.

The quaint Connecticut town was full of little shops and things to do, surrounded by nature and water every step of the way; farms, beaches and marinas on Long Island Sound, streams, Mill River, Lake Mohegan, The Cascades.

Coming up on one of those shopping plazas, Jillian was met with a traffic jam up ahead. A car was sitting so far over the line it nearly blocked both lanes. Car horns blasted. They crept around the monstrosity on both sides, dodging oncoming traffic to get by, without stopping to help. The right turning lane was a rubber-necking back-up. By the time Jillian was able to pass, she saw who it was. She pulled up along-side and stopped. Grandma.

She was so far over the line that Jillian opened her driver's side window and tapped on the passenger-side of Grandma's window. Grandma didn't find this odd. She was so happy to see her, she waved frantically. Maybe Jillian was a long-lost friend she hadn't seen in years. Jillian bit her lip. Grandma seemed completely unaware that this was a problem and didn't know what to do when the light turned green.

Jillian motioned Grandma on and she waved goodbye with a smile. She snuck in behind to follow her. Grandma drove aimlessly, slowing at the first few driveway entrances and then speeding up to the next driveway, cutting off cars as they passed her thinking she was going to turn in. She eventually pulled into a lot she would normally not stop in since she had fallen there decades ago. Shaw's.

Jillian approached the car. "Grandma, what are you doing?"

Grandma looked confused and scared. "I'm just out for a drive."

"Grandma ... " Jillian sounded like she was speaking to a child. Grandma was caught.

She sighed. "I'm trying to find Friendly's, but I got lost."

"Friendly's is right around the corner." Grandma stretched her neck to the left to see. "The other corner."

"Oh, you're right."

Grandma had been driving to Friendly's since Jillian was a child.

"I'll just go into Fairway Beef for a few things."

"Grandma, remember? Fairway Beef closed." She looked like it was the worst thing she had ever heard; her eyes started to well up.

"Fine, I'll go to A&P then."

"I'm sorry," Jillian felt bad, "the A&P isn't there anymore either."

Finally, Grandma looked at the plaza she was in. She stared up at the sign that clearly read, "Shaw's" and with a confused look called the store by one of its former names, "Edwards".

"I'll go in with you."

Traveling at a snail's pace, they finally made it down aisle one and up the middle of aisle two. Painfully slow, yet apparently more physically painful than Grandma had let on. Grandma held onto the carriage, sciatic pain shot down to her leg. She was adamant about not having surgery to fix it. Tears streamed down her face from the pain. Jillian was torn between staying with her to make sure she was ok or somehow making the shopping experience quicker.

"Grandma, let's go home, I'll finish the shopping later."

"NO."

Jillian was taken aback by her decisiveness. She didn't know what to do. "Grandma, I'm going to go look for bread." Jillian left Grandma in the middle of aisle two, ran to get a cart and flew through the next several aisles getting their necessities for the week, including a container of fudge swirl ice cream. Grandma seemed pleased. She rested in Jillian's car while she packed it up and they left to go home. Grandma didn't remember she had driven her own car.

*

Dad handed Jillian the key to the car. Her mother watched.

"Car's back in the garage."

"Thanks," Jillian said to her dad. "It's time," she said to her mother.

"I know what we need to do … I just can't do it," her mother said.

"It's dangerous. What if she gets lost and no one's there to help her? What if her sciatic nerve acts up and she can't hit the brake? What if she drives off the road, or gets stuck somewhere, or causes an accident?" Jillian threw her hands up in the air.

"I can't. Not yet."

"Mom. I get that the car is a big deal for her."

"No, Jillian, you don't." Her mother always had a way of making her feel like a child. "Grandpa taught Grandma how to drive. He pulled that car so far up into the breezeway that even he didn't think she'd be able to back out. But you know what? She did it.

48

She proved him wrong. And because of that he *'let'* her drive the car. And from that moment on, that car was her freedom."

Jillian pictured the car in the breezeway and her grandfather swearing up a storm as she tried to concentrate.

"That car ..." her mother pointed in the direction of the garage "it is her independence."

"That car ..." Jillian pointed too, "is a danger now."

"What if she cries that we took her car away?"

"What if we don't?"

Jillian trudged up the stairs to her loft. Dad stayed to finish up some maintenance on Grandma's yard and went upstairs when he was done. Her mother followed.

Her parents stood in the doorway. "We're concerned about Grandma."

"Yeah, I've been telling you, she's getting pretty forgetful."

"Do you know what she's doing downstairs right now?"

"Oh God, Mom, weren't you watching her while Dad was outside? I can *never* get a break. It's *always* me. What is she doing?"

"No, it's ok, nothing bad. Just go see."

Jillian ran down the stairs.

"Hi," Grandma mumbled with a mouth full of something ... gloppy.

"I see you're eating a bowl of your favorite cornflakes, but what the…" Jillian stopped herself. Grandma, revealed a gluey grin. "Grandma, what is that? Is the milk bad?" asked Jillian, worried.

"No, it's cream cheese."

"Cream cheese? What on earth?"

"Yeah," Grandma was proud.

Jillian peered in for a closer look. "You're supposed to have milk with that. Wait a minute. That's not cream cheese, it's ... Oh it's sour cream." Jillian cringed. "Why do you have sour cream on it? And you have enough sugar on that for ten bowls of cereal. Here, let me get you a fresh bowl with milk."

"No, I like it like this."

"I'll get you a new bowl of cornflakes with *milk*." She reached into the fridge. "How did I forget the milk?"

"No, it all comes from the same place anyway. It's white."

"This is true," Jillian reluctantly agreed, forcing the worry away from her eyes.

"Don't frown. You'll get wrinkles. It takes more muscles to frown than it does to smile. So you might as well smile."

"Ok Grandma," Jillian conceded, pouring a glass of juice and kissing her on the cheek.

"I have to run out again for milk, I'll be right back. Don't move, ok?"

"We're taking off too," her dad said.

"Can you wait until I come back?"

"Grandma will be fine." Jillian's mother continued. "She's had enough excitement for the day. She won't go anywhere. You won't be gone long anyway."

Jillian grabbed her keys and looked around the neighborhood as she drove. She thought about how many times she had driven to the corner of Stillson and Black Rock Turnpike since she was a child. The Angus Steakhouse on the right hand corner and old Moishes deli on the left after the bank. She remembered her mother and Grandma having to be first in line on chilly mornings for holiday specialties like smoked and fresh kielbasa. She remembered the snap of the casing bursting in her mouth paired with the smooth creaminess of Grandma's mashed "pa-tay-tas". It had been quite some time since Grandma had remembered how to cook anything. Her recipe book was out on the counter just a few holidays earlier, although she knew these recipes backward and forward. No one recognized it as a sign.

At the corner convenience store, Jillian ran to the back, grabbing the milk off the shelf like a child with someone else's money, quickly checking the expiration date. She tapped her foot in line while a wrinkly woman took her time choosing the perfect menthol and pack of gum to cover it up. Jillian wanted to nudge her.

On the way back, Jillian slowed to the stop sign on the corner of Sterner, but it was gone. It had been plowed down. Part of the fence was down too. Jillian swallowed hard and wondered how she had missed it on the way down the street just minutes earlier. *Had this happened earlier?* It couldn't have been Grandma.

Jillian's mind raced with the sounds of sirens, buzzers, beeps. She pictured Grandma in a hospital bed with nurses around her. She sped down the street, and slowed carefully into the driveway with an eerie feeling. The sunlight shone in her eyes through the windshield. She ran up the steps and into the house, forgetting to check to see if the car was in the garage.

She peeked in the window first before opening the door. She looked past the weathered metal venetian blinds and the flowing vintage handmade ruffles that adorned the sides of the window on the door. Jillian was always relieved to find Grandma sitting at the kitchen table, but she wasn't there.

Jillian creeked open the door. "Grandma?" No answer. Her bowl and glass were on the table. The house was silent with the exception of the ticking of a wrought iron clock and her own heart beating. Jillian threw her things down on the table and ran into the next room.

She wasn't on her chair in the living room, she wasn't lying on the floor. Jillian moved through the living room, willing to hear a sound, a movement. "Grandma," Jillian called out, but heard nothing. She wasn't in the bathroom. Jillian snuck quietly into her bedroom. She wasn't in bed. Jillian walked around to the foot of the bed, and stopped for a moment before looking over the edge. "Grandma?" Nothing. She took a deep breath. She wasn't on the floor on the other side of the bed.

Jillian straightened up and ran down the hall to the den. She stopped short of the doorway, ready to find her on the floor when she saw her lying on the daybed looking her way. "There you are." She wasn't moving. "Grandma?" Grandma was motionless but her eyes were open. Jillian held her breath and approached the bed, saying her name a little louder this time. "Grandma." Nothing. Not a movement, not a breath. Jillian was hesitant to get closer. She stood looking down at Grandma, peacefully still. Her stomach sickened. *Please don't be dead. Please don't be dead. Oh God.* "Grandma," Jillian shouted at her. Nothing. "Grandma?" she toned it down, like a whiny child about to cry. She bit her lip and hoped it wasn't true. *Oh my God, Oh my God.* The tears started. Jillian clenched her chest and tried not to hyperventilate. "Grand.

Maaa!"

"Whaaaat," Grandma answered, startled and annoyed.

"Ahhhhhh," Jillian stood frozen, eyes wide.

"Ahhhhhh," Grandma screamed.

"Why are you screaming?"

"Why are YOU screaming?" Grandma screamed.

"Why didn't you answer me?"

"I was lying on my good ear."

"You were looking at me."

"I was sleeping."

"Your eyes were open."

"I sleep with my eyes open."

"What?"

"I sleep with my eyes open."

"Shit."

"Don't do it there," Grandma joked.

"That should have been something that someone TOLD ME. You. Scared. Me. I thought you were dead."

"Well you almost DID scare me to death." They laughed and hugged and Jillian cried and laughed all over again.

"I love you so much, Grandma."

"I love you too Jillie-Bean."

"Now go back to bed. You feel ok? "

"I'm fine ... now."

Jillian gave her a look and left the room shaking her head.

-Chapter Fifteen-

"The car won't start."

"Ok, we'll look into it."

Again. "The car won't start."

"Ok, we'll look into it."

This appeased Grandma for a few weeks until she called Mac, the long-time family mechanic, to come to the house. Somehow she remembered who to call and remembered her own address. He looked under the hood and Grandma inspected.

"Ah," he found the problem quickly and held the unplugged spark plug in his hand. "Oh." He adjusted his glasses with his grease-stained fingers for a closer look. "It seems —"

"Is it bad?" Grandma peered at the part.

"Well, I'ma gonna have to special order some parts for that thing-a-ma-bobber there. It may take a few days up to a week. Just be patient, it will take a little while." Grandma pretended she understood.

A few hours later, Grandma called Mac at the gas station.

"Ah, yes, this is Heloise on Sterner Road. Just seein' if the parts came in for my car." Her speech whistled because she didn't have her teeth in.

"Hi Heloise. It will take just a few more days. Can I call you when it's in?" Again, that appeased her until the next time she called. It didn't matter if she called two days later, or two minutes later. Jillian had informed Mac and his assistants about Grandma's dementia so they always knew what to say. Eventually she stopped asking about the car.

*

Jillian brought Grandma shopping and to all of her doctor's appointments over the course of the next several months. While Jillian drove through Fairfield, she was flooded with memories of her childhood. She remembered the smell and buttery feel of the expensive leather "pocketbooks" versus the cheap plastic ones at Howland's. She remembered begging Grandma for relish at Kuhn's hotdog stand; the soggy bun turning the consistency of school glue. She never ordered relish again.

-*Chapter Sixteen*-

Over the next few weeks, the official diagnosis of Alzheimer's made its way on paper. Grandma became argumentative about everything from eating, to cleaning, to leaving the house.

"Jillie, What are you doing?"

"I'm washing the floor."

"I washed it yesterday."

Jillian looked around. "No, you didn't."

"Yes, I did." Like everything else, it became an argument. Grandma was adamant that she was capable and lucid enough to know that she washed the floor yesterday.

Another argument that came up a lot was, "Why are you vacuuming? I vacuumed yesterday." Grandma really thought she had touched a vacuum at all in the last year.

"OK." Jillian tried to avoid an argument.

Waiting for Grandma to go to bed seemed like forever. She became like a toddler, using all the same stall tactics. "Can I have water? I'm very, very hungry. I have to go to the bathroom. I'm not tired. Why do I have to go to bed?"

When Grandma finally fell asleep, Jillian would fire up the nineteen-eighties upright vacuum cleaner and push it around the house hoping Grandma wouldn't wake up. When she got to the doorway of Grandma's room, she peeked in, took a deep breath and ran around the room. Grandma didn't so much as stir or stop snoring. Mission accomplished.

*

One Saturday afternoon another argument ensued. "Here. Take your medicine."

"No. I don't need it"

"Doctor D. says you do, it will help your memory."

"My memory is just fine."

Patti gave a quick knock and walked in the door. "Hey," they exchanged hellos. She leaned in to kiss Grandma on the cheek; Grandma recoiled.

"Grammy, I'm Patti, remember me?"

Grandma wasn't buying it.

"It's me. I'm Patti."

"If you say so."

Jillian was pleased that Grandma still knew *her*. She never expected the day would come when she wouldn't know her.

Patti looked like she was about to cry. "What're you up to?"

"I'm just trying to get Grandma to take her medicine."

"Grammy, you know the medicine is supposed to help."

"She's trying to poison me."

Patti gasped. Jillian rolled her eyes. "No one's trying to poison you. Just take this."

Grandma took the medicine with some coaxing, she squinted at them as if she was watching their every move.

Later that week, Jillian found something new in the bottom of the drawer, a pile of shriveled medicine capsules. She'd been pretending to take this medicine and spitting it out. *How did she ... ?*

*

Jillian was awakened by the creak of the floorboard outside of Grandma's room and the click of her walker. *Why is she up now?*

She heard Grandma exploring her way down the hallway to

56

the bathroom, stopping to smooth her hand over the wall to search for the light. Jillian shot out of bed and ran downstairs in time to see her still walking toward the bathroom. She could see a wet spot on the back of her purple sweat pants.

"Grandma ... Grandma." Grandma tried to maneuver her walker around in the tiny bathroom. She didn't have her hearing aid in. "Grandma!"

Startled, she turned her head toward the door.

"After you sit down I'll help you get changed."

"What?"

"Sit down on the toilet and I'll help you get changed."

"I want to wear these."

"They're wet."

"That's because I spilled."

"No, I don't think so." Jillian went to the next room to replace the purple sweat suit with a clean teal set. Grandma was already walking out of the bathroom but Jillian was trying to redirect her back in. "Go back in, you're wet. I'll help you take your pants off."

"WHAT?" Grandma shouted.

"I'll help you take your pants off."

"NO. I'm not wet."

"Yes you are."

"No, I'm not."

"Then what's the wet spot?"

"I spilled."

"So it's wet then." Jillian tried to reason with her.

Grandma said, "No" like a stubborn toddler. "I'm not a — "

"Yes you are." Jillian interrupted before she heard her grandmother say the word "baby".

"I'm not a baby," Grandma repeated. It was nearly a whisper.

They were eye to eye. "No." Jillian paused. "No you're not. But we're not going back to bed until you change."

Growing tired, Grandma finally agreed. "Fine. Jackass."

Jillian couldn't help but laugh. This was a woman who never swore a day in her life. "Now we know how you really feel," she said under her breath. She pulled the toilet seat cover down and had her sit there and wait there until the bed was changed. It became a nightly routine for the next three nights until her mother thought to deliver a package of adult pull-ups. "Put these on."

"I'm not a baby."

*

Jillian rolled her eyes. Tonight, she would be ready for her. Jillian waited in her crisp white comforter and heavenly pillow. A smile formed on her lips. Grandma was safe in bed. She listened for her to fall asleep and then she dozed off to sleep herself, knowing she had done her job. She slept lightly with one ear out to hear when Grandma got up to go to the bathroom. She planned to wake every fifteen minutes to check the time.

The clock struck three and like a tired child emerging from bed, Grandma arose slowly and slid her feet into her pink slippers. Music swelled in Jillian's mind as she wrote the scene in her head: Grandma dawdled down the hall. She could calculate the distance from the rooms by listening for the click of the walker between the thread bare throw rugs and the hardwood floors. It signaled how much time Jillian had to get downstairs. But Jillian didn't hear any of it. She was sound asleep, dreaming it was happening.

Jillian rustled, still dreaming about Grandma waking up and what she would do. A few seconds later, Grandma smashed her body down on the toilet seat, the lid echoed a hollow ceramic sound as she landed. Jillian shot out of bed. *She's in the bathroom!* By the time Jillian got downstairs, Grandma was already coming out, yet her pants were wet, again. It was a huge fight to get her back in, and turn her around with the walker in the closet-sized bathroom.

"I already went."

"You're wet."

"No. I'm not."

"Your pants are wet. Let me change you."

"No. I'm not a baby." Grandma let out a high-pitched squeal like a toddler. "Get out." She growled.

Jillian took a step back. "Grandma, I'm trying to help you."

"I don't need help."

"Feel your pants," Jillian tried again unsuccessfully to reason with her. She didn't know what else to do except to finish what she was doing. She grabbed hold of the overfilled pull-ups and dragged them down exposing her.

"911."

"No, shhhhh, you'll wake the neighbors. I'm trying to help you," Jillian reached to pull her legs out of the pee-stenched sweat pants. "There's diarrhea, too." Great. "I need to clean you."

"No."

"Yes."

"I'm clean."

"You're not, you pooped."

"I did NOT poop."

"You did, see, it's smudged."

"That wasn't me."

"Right, must have been someone else. Let me wipe you."

Her grandmother's fingernails dug into her skin.

"Oww, Grandma, stop."

"You Stop. Help, 911."

"Stop it. Quiet."

"Help, 911."

"Ow!" Grandma was pulling Jillian's hair out in chunks. "Grandma, stop!" Tears streamed down her face.

After cleaning Grandma and tucking her back in bed, Jillian trudged upstairs. That evening marked a change; this became a typical and exhausting routine.

Jillian got into bed unable to sleep. Journal in hand, pen at the ready, but no words came. She tilted her head back onto the head-board, squeezed the bridge of her nose, either to block the tears or to urge them to fall. She inhaled. This was the responsibility she had acquired. She prayed for the confidence she needed to contin-ue on.

Eventually, Jillian bought a baby monitor so she could hear

when Grandma got out of bed. It stopped most of the battle which was getting her back in the bathroom when she thought she had already gone. When she heard Grandma getting up, she could get down the stairs and make it to the bathroom first with towels and washcloths and a fresh pull-up in hand.

Sometimes Grandma would sit and pee on her pants like a potty training toddler, so it became a routine for Jillian to pull Grandma's pants down, wipe, sponge clean, pull the sweat pants and soiled pull-ups off and slide new ones on. Getting a nightgown on her was impossible and once they allowed her to wear her sweats to bed, that argument stopped. Her bra, that was a no-go, ever, so Jillian was relieved when her mother bought her a loose fitting sports bra that she never had to take off until bath and laundry time. It fixed the fight about getting changed. The exercise bra was soft enough to sleep in and provided enough support to keep on during the day, they did not have to worry about taking it off.

Each night, Jillian snuck out to make the bed, calculating the time it would take for Grandma to leave the bathroom and get to the bedroom. She smoothed her hand over the sheets and was surprised that everything was still clean and dry for the first time in months. Memories began to flood in of so many things. She remembered the feel of the crisp sheets and the smell after Grandma hung them in the fresh breeze. She remembered the fun times of younger days.

Jillian finished straightening the blankets when Grandma came in. She was quiet, timid even. Jillian lifted her legs up into the bed to help alleviate some of her pain, and tucked her in with a kiss on the cheek. Grandma smiled and Jillian's heart broke for her.

"Jillian?"

"Yeah?" Jillian wasn't sure if Grandma was asking if it was her or if she knew it was her.

"Jillian, thank you."

Jillian choked out "you're welcome". Sadness filled her eyes; a sadness for the past and whatever was going to come. "Always." Jillian smiled, although she knew Grandma couldn't hear her.

When Jillian went back upstairs and got settled in her bed, she heard a long, drawn out fart over the baby monitor. Jillian rolled her eyes, too exhausted to find it funny. *Seriously? I just changed her. Unless she gets up, I'm not going through that again.* She didn't get up.

A few minutes later, Jillian was drifting off to sleep, but she was startled when she heard Grandma talking. She sat up in bed. *Who is she talking to?* Jillian struggled to hear what Grandma was saying over the sound of her own nervous heartbeat.

"God, are you there? Please, please, please come down and take me. I'm ready. I don't want to live like this anymore. I don't want to be sick. I can't remember anything. I'm scared. I don't know how to do things. I don't want to be a burden. I don't want to fall and crack my head open to die alone until I'm found. I want to die peacefully in my sleep in my bed. Please, please, please God. Please come down and take me. I'm ready. Please God! Please!" Grandma sobbed.

Jillian stared at the monitor, sobbing herself. *Oh God. Please. This is awful. She doesn't deserve this. No one does. Please answer her.* Jillian, like Grandma, waited for God's response. She strained to hear something; a voice, a melody, a bird. Instead the monitor squealed while Grandma pleaded, "Pleee-eeeease Gah-aaaad" and began to sob louder. Jillian put her face in her hands and inhaled sharply. After wiping her eyes, and swallowing hard, she fumbled to turn the monitor off, mostly to cry herself, but also to give them their privacy. *Maybe God won't answer if he knows I'm listening. Grandma deserves an answer. Please help her.*

*

Writing was the only thing that soothed Jillian's soul, especially when she couldn't sleep.

Let Me Comfort You
Let yourself scream, I'll hear you.
Let yourself run, I'll keep up.
Let yourself sleep, I'll hold you.
Let me be there for you.
Let yourself cry, I don't mind.
Let yourself go, I'm your strength.
Let yourself hide, I'll hide with you.
Let me comfort you.

If You Remembered Me
If you remembered me,
You'd know we had a great story.
That we used to love each other
And look out for one another.

If you remembered me,
You'd know me as your friend.
Always amazed
We could laugh for days on end.

How did you end up this way, forgetting all about today
When you remembered yesterday?
How can you look straight through me
And not know anything about me.

You're in a trance, I can't get through.
You can't see it's me you're looking through.
How can you not see me when I'm standing right here

Calm down and see me, don't be afraid, I'm right here.

We used to laugh and now I cry.
We used to sing and have a good time.
We used to go places and not have to worry.
We used to, we used to, we ...

We knew what might happen down the road
But never expected it would come.
Knocking loudly, we had no choice but to get the door.
The rest is all a blur.

Your memory was taken before our eyes.
It happened without thought despite our tries.
And when you did not know me anymore
That's when I knew it was over.

So I cried for you but mostly cried for me.
I knew it would happen, but wasn't ready
Because when it did, I couldn't believe my eyes.
And all I could think was that I needed more time.

So I'll leave the light on for you
Because I'm still waiting for you to remember me,
Remember us.
Remember you.
Remember we.

If you remembered me.

- Chapter Seventeen -

Jillian walked up the porch stairs and pressed the doorbell. Instead of a chime, a chorus of Ave Maria played until she could hear rustling inside. Jillian smiled to remember it. A woman in a muu-muu and day coat, and a man in khaki slacks, a checkered sweater, and wire-rimmed glasses answered the door.

"Hi, I'm Jillian, your neighbor."

"Jillian, I know who you are, I've known you since you were just born. I've known your mommy since she was a little girl. Arthur, look, it's Jillian Louise Sebastien, Heloise's granddaughter."

"Hi Mr. and Mrs. James." And in that moment she was eight years old, sitting on the musty basement couch with all the kids for a family photo. She hadn't been called by her full name since she was a child.

"Come in, come in. Would you like a butterscotch candy, dear, or a vanilla cream cookie?"

"No thanks."

"Are you sure?"

"Well, maybe a cookie." Jillian's mouth actually watered for it. She could remember the cookies, the taste, right down to the texture of the scalloped edges on her tongue. She even remembered the painted flower on the yellow cookie jar where they were hidden in plain view on the top shelf of the pantry resting on the crinkly contact paper.

Mr. James handed her a cookie. She bit down on the cookie

and tried to hold in her disgust with a smile. The cookie was soft, stale, not like she remembered. It very well could have been in the jar since the last time she was there, possibly the mid-eighty's.

"Here, come, have a seat." Mr. James motioned toward the pristine living room they were never allowed in growing up. Jillian could see it from the hallway, and she was still programmed with the fear of God to ever set foot in the room. "How have you been? How's Heloise?"

"Well, that's why I'm here," Jillian said. She nonchalantly grabbed a tissue from a dusty crocheted covered box and spit out the cookie, inconspicuously folding it in her palm.

"Is she ok dear?" They stopped, realizing Jillian wasn't there for a casual visit.

"Grandma's dementia is getting worse, she has Alzheimer's." Jillian tried to brush the cookie remnants that were in her mouth with her tongue. "If you see her wandering the neighborhood please call me. Oh also, if you hear someone screaming 911 and my car's in the driveway, just know that she's ok."

"Awww, H.E. double hockey sticks, that's too bad."

"Arthur, hush."

"I'm sorry dear," Mrs. James told Jillian. "We haven't seen her around, so we thought it may have been something like that. We stopped by a while back but she didn't seem to recognize us and we were too heartsick to go back. What can we do to help?" Mrs. James reached into her daycoat for a tissue to dab her nose. "Do you want a lemonade or tea Jillian?"

"No thanks, Mrs. James, I need to see Mr. and Mrs. Davie also. Then I need to make sure Grandma is okay."

"We can go there so you can talk to the Davie's."

"That might just confuse her." She hugged and waved goodbye and another sadness came over her. *This could be the last time.*

Jillian decided to take the short cut past the hedges, past the snowball bushes and under the low hanging trees. Pine, sweet lilac and apples comforted her senses and memories rushed in from the past. *Grandpa, can you cut apples with your pocketknife and can we eat them in the breezeway? Please? Grandma, do we have to help Grandpa rake the apples today? I'm getting a blister.*

She saw visions of her childhood, playing with her neighborhood friends, taking turns around the yard on the riding lawnmover. *Grandpa, Go faster! My legs are burning and my eyes are tearing from fumes. You want to stop? No!* Jillian would sing loudly at the top of her lungs until Grandpa turned the engine off and she would stop singing. *Next!* And a different kid would be hoisted up for a painful, yet exhilarating ride around the yard. Inevitably, someone would do something to annoy Grandpa and the neighbor's could hear his expletives booming throughout the neighborhood, but all-in-all, many memories were made on Sterner Road.

Jumping in and out of the plastic kiddie pool summer after summer was a favorite pastime. They were always yelled at for running in and out and filling the pool with mud and grass; the grass that stuck to their legs and cheeks; the grass that tattled on them when they said they didn't do it. Memories of running full speed ahead, drenched in sweat, all summer long were more accurate. They rested only to catch their breath in the shade for mere seconds. "You're going to catch a cold, you're soaked." Grandma would say. The kids would shout back, "Grandma, it's summer."

Jillian remembered Grandpa working on the garden from morning to night. Shovels, hoes, fence, sticks, string and vegetables. It spanned the entire backyard then. Big Boy tomatoes or was it Big Girls and Better Boys? Grandpa had every variety including Steak, Beef and Cherry. Jillian remembered the tomatoes had weird names and could never keep them straight.

Time was spent snapping beans into a metal colander and pulling carrots out from the root, usually needing help. Big peppers, little peppers, green, red, yellow peppers, cucumbers, he tried potatoes but they didn't taste good, long, sleek eggplant, even sunflowers and leafy lettuce. The kids would complain, "Grandpa, we got enough vegetables to come outta our ears." He would say, "Don't complain, when I was your age, we had no food to eat."

The homemade zucchini bread was a staple from the large harvest. But so was mushy cooked squash. They were forced to eat the watery, butter-drenched lumps that were splattered on their plates. Just the thought of steaming simmered squash seeds made Jillian want to heave.

Jillian remembered hiding behind the blackberry and raspberry bushes, dirty fingers, sneaking berries, seeing how long it would take Grandpa to start yelling. "Son's-a-bitches, get outta there, don't touch the berries". The juice deliciously dripped down their wrists as they ran away across the yard laughing for being caught.

She remembered tripping over mounds and holes where the moles caused havoc on the yard and Grandpa trying to "smoke 'em out" with sticks of dynamite. If the animal rights people were around then, they'd surely have a problem with it. "You kids go in the house, Ima gonna light this stick-a-dynamite." And all the kids would run into the house and fight for a window-seat in hopes of seeing flying mole guts or at least some fur.

Jillian remembers asking, "Grandma, do you have a jar? We're collecting bugs."

"You're NOT bringing bugs into the house."

Or the time they shouted, "Grandma, we ate mushrooms we found."

"From where?"

"The yard!"

"Get in the tub. Get the Ipecac," rang throughout the neighborhood.

When Jillian got to the back of Grandma's house, worry and reality set in. She wasn't ten anymore and Alzheimer's was completely taking over their lives. Jillian caught a glimpse of something under the bathroom window. It looked like ... "What is that? Laundry?" Jillian said outloud. It was something yellowed, white? Muddy from being outside. *What the hell? Soiled underwear. She's throwing dirty underwear out the window? Why the hell would she do that? She's reverted, worse than a child, no common sense whatsoever.* Jillian shook her head and shrugged her shoulders, picking up the dirty underwear with a stick. *What's next?* Jillian was afraid to ask.

-*Chapter Eighteen*-

Jillian got a whiff of Grandma that took her aback. "Did you take a shower yesterday?"

"I took a shower this morning"

"I don't think you did."

"I'm not a baby".

Jillian couldn't remember the last time she saw Grandma in freshly washed pin-curls and a hand towel clothes-pinned around her neck.

Jillian marched into the bathroom. She looked around for any evidence of a recent shower. There was no water pooled around the drain. There was no puddle in the soap dish, no mushy soap, instead a crusty slice of green soap that looked crackled, shriveled and stringy like someone had run a lemon zester over it. There was no towel in the hamper and she was wearing the same outfit she had been changed into.

Jillian looked around the light blue tiled bathroom with the red carpet and red yarn toilet lid cover for a way to prove that Grandma had taken a shower. She moved the curtain out of place. No. She could get annoyed and move it back, then I'd have no proof. She thought about taking the Jean Naté scented powder puff from the circular yellow container on the top of the toilet and leaving some powder in the tub. Grandma would see it and wash it down the drain, then Jillian would never know for sure.

Then, Jillian snatched one square off the toilet paper roll and ripped off two quarter-sized sections, careful not to make them too big and noticeable, yet not too small. She placed them in the tub, one near the drain and one near the soap. If the water was turned on, the paper would move, shrivel, gunk up, something.

Later that day, Jillian checked.

"Grandma, you need to shower."

"I took a shower this morning."

"No you didn't."

"I'm not a baby."

After three to four days of the Grandma you need to shower conversation, the toilet paper was still intact. Jillian called her mother.

"Mom. I can't do this anymore. I'm doing things that a grand-daughter shouldn't be doing. You need to help me. You're the daughter. You need to come help."

When Jillian's mother arrived, she was appalled by the stench. She stripped Grandma down kicking, spitting, hitting, screaming to get her in the shower and hose her down as quickly as possible. Was she afraid of the water? What was the problem? The you-can't-make-me-take-a-shower-when-I-already-took-one fight was exhausting and nearly impossible.

Soon, Jillian's mother showed up to bathe Grandma daily. She brought a handicap shower bench, and a hand-held faucet that Jillian's father installed. Jillian was glad to have someone else take over although it was difficult to listen to the screaming from the other side of the door.

"Jackass!" Grandma screamed.

At least I'm not the only jackass in the house. Jillian chuckled.

One morning Jillian helped her mother peel Grandma's sweat-shirt off when she saw the bruise on her arm. It was the size of an orange. Jillian inhaled sharply and stared at her mother for an answer.

Her mother didn't say anything.

Jillian felt sick to her stomach and pushed past her mother. She ran down the stairs to the basement to get the towels from the dryer. She couldn't hold back her anger. She screamed and smashed her hands on the lid of the dryer. She forced the tears back.

When she returned to the bathroom, she draped a warm towel around Grandma's neck so she was able to cover herself up while she sat on the bath bench. The handheld water was still an issue, and getting her in the tub was a fight, but the warmth comforted her and even brought a smile briefly to her face. Keeping her covered up eased her and bath time was a tiny bit easier for the moment. When the towel got soaked and heavy and she had to expose herself, another screaming fit ensued but at that point bath time was over anyway.

"Time's up. Let's get out," her mother said.

"You get out." Grandma said.

Jillian smirked and rolled her eyes.

After Grandma was settled back into bed, Jillian met her mother at the kitchen table. Her mother's clothes were soaked. Jillian's hands were clasped around a reheated cup of tea. "What are we going to do?" They stared at each other in silence.

- Chapter Nineteen -

Several companions were introduced over the course of the next few weeks, but they hadn't worked out. In fact, they were simply awful. They either didn't know what to do for Grandma, were too pushy, were being paid to watch TV or stay on their phones, or simply were not a good match. The sight of some of them would agitate her and Jillian didn't even feel comfortable leaving the house. Phone calls were made, and paperwork was shuffled. Everyone was at their wit's end before the heavens opened up and sent Mabel.

*

Mabel was a Jamaican beauty in her early thirties with a smooth complexion and sparkling white teeth. Her caring nature emanated around her with scents of cocoa butter and jasmine.

"Grandma, Mabel will be staying with you today. You met her last week." Jillian expected a reaction.

Grandma nodded without words.

"OK." Jillian tried to break the silence.

"Alrighty, Miss Jillian. Mrs. Heloise." Mabel clapped her hands together, ready to start her day. She headed toward the pack of cards on the table. Grandma hadn't played cards in ages. "I've got this. Go. Off to class with your pretty little self. Get lost after university for a while. We will be fine." Mabel took the elastic band off of the deck.

Jillian shrugged her shoulders. "OK … are you sure?"

"Yes ma'am. I've been a caregiver for many years, 'Mon. Your Grandma will be fine."

Jillian said her goodbyes. "I'm going to class. See you later."

"Remember, don't rush back dear."

Jillian meandered after class, not knowing what to do with herself. She continued home. To her relief, Grandma had tolerated Mabel and no one looked frazzled when she returned.

The following day was a bit different.

"Grandma, Mabel is here."

Grandma walked past her pushing her walker. Tennis balls made the walker quieter and easier to push since she had either become too tired to lift it or had forgotten how to use it. Grandma looked at Mabel as she passed by. "Jackass."

Mabel threw her head back and laughed.

Jillian apologized.

Grandma lifted up the walker and tried to smash Mabel's toe with it. Mabel side-stepped out of the way, but something was behind her smile like: Is this the kind of a day we're going to have? I accept your challenge. Bring it lady.

"Jillian, you best be on your way to finish your studies." Mabel turned on the faucet.

Jillian was hesitant. She wasn't used to someone helping or spending time with Grandma while she was home, or at all for that matter.

"I got this." She shooed Jillian on and put a glass of water on the table for Grandma.

*

Between classes or school holidays Jillian still brought Grandma to all her doctor's appointments, so Mabel had time off on these days and the weekends. On this particular day, Jillian decided to stop at the grocery store on the way back.

"Let's just run in for a minute."

"No."

"What'dya mean, 'no'?"

"I'm not going."

"You have to go, it will only take a minute."

"No. Eeeeeeeeeeeeeee." She screamed a piercing screech that went up in decibels.

"Shhhhh. You want to stay in the car?"

"Yes."

"OK, fine. I'll only be a minute. The temp is comfortable in here. Keep the windows up and the doors locked."

Jillian ran through the store on high adrenaline, not wanting to leave Grandma for too long in the car. She raced through the aisles grabbing what she needed before getting in the express lane. The woman behind her was invading her personal space, practically parallel with her as if Jillian wouldn't notice she was trying to cut the line.

"Ex-cuuuse me," Jillian couldn't help herself.

The woman huffed and backed up to give Jillian some space.

On the way out, the sun reflected on the windshield, and Jillian couldn't see Grandma sitting there. The passenger side door was wide open. Jillian dug the balls of her feet into the pavement and started running like a maniac toward the car. Grandma was not there. She wasn't in or near the car. She wasn't in the backseat. She wasn't lying on the ground near the car, she wasn't behind the car or around the other side. Jillian dropped the grocery bag by the car and scanned the lot. Then with a knot in her stomach she scanned the double-lined road to make sure Grandma wasn't wandering toward traffic like a child. There was no sign of her.

"Grandma, Grandma," Jillian shouted through the parking lot.

"Are you lost?" a stranger replied.

"NO, but my grandmother is."

"What does she look like?"

"Like a lost grandmother," Jillian snapped back. She scanned the parking lot again, turning around a like a top, getting herself dizzy. Everything was spinning. She tried to catch her balance and ran back inside.

Jillian interrupted everyone and pushed to the front of the customer service line. "I lost my grandmother, she has dementia."

Jillian started to sweat and tears formed in her eyes.

"Oh dearie, we'll help you find her," said the plump woman behind the counter with the way-too-short-to-be-permed hair. Her expression morphed from processing what Jillian had said to comprehension. Worry rippled over her face. "I'll help. I'm Madge. What was she wearing dear?"

"She's in a tan sweater, glasses and brown loafers."

"I'm going to check the aisles," Jillian shouted out as she ran down the length of the store looking down each aisle, seeing nobody that resembled Grandma. A crackle came over the intercom system and someone blew into it before speaking.

"Attention customers." Madge cleared her throat into the microphone. "Grandma in a tan sweater, glasses, and brown loafers please come to the customer service station. Your granddaughter is looking for you. Grandma in a tan sweater, glasses, and brown loafers please come to the customer service station. Your granddaughter is looking for you."

Jillian circled back to the customer service desk, out of breathe. Grandma was not there.

"Anything?" Madge asked her.

"Nothing." Jillian ran past to check the first few aisles and the produce/deli/bakery area. No Grandma. Sharp pains jabbed her stomach from worry. When she got back, two other Grandma's and even a Grandpa in tan sweaters stood by the customer service desk waiting to be chosen by a granddaughter, but none of them was Jillian's. "I don't know what to do. I'm going to look again outside and maybe the area stores in the plaza." Jillian turned to leave the building, as a police officer approached the customer service desk.

"This is the young woman who lost her grandmother," Madge said to him, directing a long, red fingernail her way.

"Can you describe to me what happened?" The officer escorted her out of the building. Jillian looked back at Madge and threw out a 'thank you' over her shoulder.

Outside, Jillian scanned the lot again.

"Officer Smith to Station 3, We got a 10-57 missing person, Shaw's parking lot ... What was she wearing?"

Jillian couldn't think.

"Why don't you go home and wait for her?"

"What? What if she comes back here? What if she looks for my car?"

"Ma'am, it is our experience that dementia and Alzheimer's patients typically try to make their way home."

Jillian felt like a reprimanded child. "She won't remember how to get home and it's too far for her to walk."

"And you were on your way back from a doctor's office and you left her in the car."

"She didn't want to come in."

"Did you try to have her come in with you?"

"Yes, of course I did. She didn't want to."

"UmmHmmm."

"What was I supposed to do? It's not like I could stick her in the cart."

Interference came over the walkie and the officer translated the jargon. "We found Grandma."

"What? Where? Is she ok?"

"She's home."

"She's home?" Jillian held her chest.

"She must have hitch-hiked."

"Hitch-hiked? She doesn't even remember where she lives."

"Do you want a ride home?"

Jillian shook her head to process it all. *How in the world?*

-Chapter Twenty-

Jillian drove home, hands shaking, clutching the wheel. She tried to exit the car before putting it in park, then pulled up loudly on the emergency brake and ran toward the door where Patti greeted her.

Jillian tried to form sentences and ask questions, but the words wouldn't come. "Patti! How did you…"

"Grandma's fine. I rushed over when I saw the police in your driveway." Patti pulled her by the elbow.

"I can't believe this."

"I know right?" They walked into the kitchen together.

"Grandma, where have YOU been?" Jillian, exasperated, threw her arms around Grandma's shoulders.

"I'm right here in my house," she stated more matter-of-factly than Jillian appreciated.

After the police left, Patti and Jillian got Grandma settled in. It wasn't difficult because she didn't remember getting lost in the first place. She had tired herself out, so while she napped Patti and Jillian hung out.

"We haven't had a girl's day in so long." Patti shook her head. "You need to get out."

"I can't leave Grandma for too long. How about tomorrow when Mabel is here?"

The next day when Jillian and Patti returned from the mall,

Grandma was standing at the stove. The house smelled familiar, warm, soothing ... rich hamburgers drenched in a thick steaming pan of creamy mushroom soup minus the mashed potatoes and French-Style canned green beans that usually went with it. Jillian and Patti looked at each other cautiously. Grandma was standing free without her walker, smiling, talking, cooking, squishing ground beef in her hands in a mixture of eggs and bread crumbs, making burgers the way she always used to.

"Oh my God," they chimed together.

"Mabel, what's going on?"

"Your Grandma made dinner all my herself."

"You didn't help?"

"No, she remembered everything on her own. It's a miracle that it is, a real miracle."

"Hi Jillie-Bean, hi Patti. I made supper."

"I see that."

Grandma shuffled over with a slight spring in her step carrying two plates to the table, walker and cane-free. "Here sit," she served the burgers proudly.

"We cannot eat this," Jillian whispered.

"We can't NOT eat it," Patti whispered back. She smiled at Grandma and winced when she wasn't looking.

"Let's pretend," Jillian nibbled a small piece of the rounded edge, like a mouse. Actually I think it's ok." The two ate like house guests being forced to sip tea from a child's play set, not knowing if the water was retrieved from the bathroom sink or the toilet.

As they ate, Grandma washed the dishes like she always had. It was like she'd snapped back to before she was sick. She was cured. But how?

"We'll clean up and get you ready for bed. Thanks so much for cooking. It was ... a nice surprise."

"Patti, dear, you should visit more often." Grandma patted her on the cheek. Mabel helped her get ready before she left for the night and Jillian and Patti chatted on the porch.

"How weird." Patti whispered while Grandma shuffled into the bedroom. "She hasn't functioned in years. Even yesterday. Do you think all that other bad memory stuff was just a fluke?"

"I hope so. I just don't understand it. I constantly worry about her and it seems like no one else does."

"I do." Patti said.

"I know you do, but you're not here. She got lost driving the other day and today she seems fine? It makes no sense. How am I to know what will set her off? I'm stuck in this role of caregiver and I can't get out. Thank God I have Mabel." Jillian smiled as Mabel heard the last part of the conversation on her way out the door.

"Grandma is safe in bed. Do you need anything while I'm here?"

"No Mabel, you've done so much! I really appreciate it."

"You know, Miss Jillian, I really love her. Thank you for choosing me to take help take care of her."

"I think you're growing on her, too!"

They waved as Mabel backed out of the driveway.

"See, Mabel is amazing," Patti said, "but she's not here all the time. And just because you're *here* doesn't mean all the responsibility should be left to you."

"Yeah, right."

"You CAN go out and have *fun*."

"I can't. I don't even like sitting out here while Grandma's inside, alone."

"She's in bed. She's fine."

"I'm just anxious, I guess." They sat and chatted for about twenty minutes.

"Shhh." Jillian put her hand up to stop Patti from talking. "Did you hear that?"

"You've got to stop this. You're going to have a stroke from stress. Grandma's fine. Do you need anything before I go?"

"No, I'm fine, thanks for spending time with me today."

"Any time." Patti gave Jillian a tight squeeze. "Sit. Relax. Enjoy the quiet."

"I will."

Patti looked her in the eyes to challenge her lie.

"What? I promise!" Jillian assured her.

After Patti left, Jillian sat back down but only for a few seconds before worry got the best of her. She nodded her head, bit her lip and popped back up. *I just need to go check on her first. Then I'll relax.*

Jillian rushed through the house toward the bedroom. *I've really got to stop this nonsense, she's sleeping.* She took a double-take at the floor beside the bed. Grandma was on the floor.

Jillian froze. "Oh my God!"

Grandma started crying. "I can't get up."

Jillian reached out for Grandma but a stench knocked her backward. Grandma was lying in a pool of diarrhea. *So much for the pull-up.* Jillian tried to console her and breathe.

"Did you hit your head? Is anything's broken?"

"I don't know but I can't get up."

"I'm going to call for help." Jillian tried to talk without choking. She gasped for air as she dialed the phone in the other room. "Dad, Grandma fell and I can't get her up, there's diarrhea everywhere, I can't breathe. Bring the steam cleaner."

Minutes later, her parents barged in. "What, did you drive over sidewalks and through red lights to get here?" But as they approached, they were hit by the wall of stench that knocked them backward, too. "I told you. Did you bring the steam cleaner?" They looked at each other, not saying anything. They tried to help her up before resorting to calling 911 to have the hospital check her out and clean her up.

"Mom, I can't do this anymore," Jillian pleaded. "I need help. You have to get me someone here full-time. She needs more care than I can give her. This isn't helping her. I'm doing more than a granddaughter should do. You need to be here or get someone here to help."

Her mother brushed it off. "It will be fine."

"Why? Why do you have to do that?"

"Do what?"

"You haven't heard a word I said. You act like you don't even care."

"I do."

"Then get me some help."

"We are helping."

"Then you need to stay here overnight."

"Don't you tell me what I need to do."

Jillian knew the conversation was over. She made her way up the stairs. The weight of disappointment made it nearly impossible to make it up the last step. She buried her head in the pillow while heavy tears of defeat pooled in the corners of her eyes before overflowing down her face. She didn't bother to wipe them away.

-Chapter Twenty-One-

Jillian tossed in her sleep for the next few nights about the decision she had to make. Thoughts echoed in her mind. *You're trying to poison me. You stole my teeth. I can't do this anymore. I need help. Don't tell me what to do. I have to go feed my grandmother. God, please come down and take me, I'm ready. If you say so. Jackass. I can't do this anymore. I can't do this anymore.* Jillian sat up and gasped. "I can't do this anymore." She yelled out loud. Jillian realized she was having a nightmare but when she woke up, her reality was clear. Grandma needed more care than she could provide. It was time for her to move out, get an apartment, enjoy life, date. Surely her mother would think she was being selfish. Jillian already felt guilty enough on her own. But it was a decision that had to be made. It wasn't helping Grandma to keep her home.

What is that noise? Is that ... scissors? Mother of ... A strange noise on the monitor woke her up from her bed in the loft. *How did she find the scissors and what in all of God's creation could she be cutting? Now? Her hair? Her fingernails? She's going to chop a finger off or poke herself in the eye. Jesus, she's become my child.*
Jillian ran down the stairs with her heart pounding in her head. The light was on in Grandma's room. Sharp metal scissors were in her hand, and a strange look took over her eyes. Fabric remnants

covered the bed.

"What are you doing?"

"Cutting a hole."

For God's Sake. "Why?"

"I'm hot."

"Just because you're hot isn't a reason to cut your new blanket."

"I don't like it."

"Give me the scissors."

"No."

"Give me the scissors."

"No. You have no right."

"You have no idea what you're doing."

"Leave me alone."

"No, this is ridiculous."

"You're ridiculous."

Oh God. "Look, Grandma, give me the scissors and go to bed. Here, I'm taking the blanket off and you can just use the sheet."

Grandma's eyes focused on Jillian. Instead of looking through her, her demeanor seemed less possessed. She snapped into reality as Jillian stood before her with her hand out.

"Oh here," she smiled. "I found some scissors, do you want them?"

Jillian rolled her eyes. "Sure." Grandma handed over the scissors and Jillian helped her into bed pulling the sheet over her.

I'll have to hide them from her like a child and make sure they're hidden every day. Scissors and stove. What's next? Jillian didn't sleep for the rest of the night.

-Chapter Twenty-Two-

"Mom," Jillian clenched the phone. "I need help."

"What's wrong."

"Mom. This. Everything. I can't do this on my own anymore. I need someone here overnight. She's up all night. And I need to move out. I need to feel like I'm in my twenties, not my eighties. I'm tired. Exhausted. This is all too much. I've done all I can for her but this has become much more than I can handle. I'm not saying that I don't *want* to do it anymore. I'm saying I *can't*."

"I understand, but you can't leave her."

"Mom."

"What?"

"That negates what you just said. No! No, you don't understand."

"Yes, we do, but she needs you."

"You just did it again. It's not really my responsibility to be primary caregiver just because I live here. I can't do it anymore. It's beyond my capability. I'm going to look for an apartment, and believe me, I've wrestled with this decision and my heart is breaking."

"You never mentioned this before."

"Mom. You don't listen. I need help."

"We help. I bathe her." Jillian's mother insisted.

"She needs more than that. *I need more than that.*"

The conversation went nowhere.

Jillian dreamed of the possibility of having a simpler life, being an actual twenty-something, having less responsibility. Although the weeks were harder with each day, it still took her another week to actually open the classified section without feeling ill. Jillian took a deep breath and dialed the number.

"Is the apartment still available? I'll be there in fifteen minutes."

She opened the door and fell in love instantly. She would have the entire floor, two bedrooms, an eat-in kitchen with antique tin ceiling tiles and a pantry, dining room, living room, washer/dryer hook-up in the basement, front porch, and back porch, too. There were large sunny windows at every glance, cherry wood beams separating the rooms. It was quiet. It was a dream.

Her palms were sweating and she kept clearing her throat. She pushed the application away when it was time to sign. "Can I have more time?"

"You can … but you run the risk that it won't be available."

She called her parents before starting the car. Her heart beat loudly as she put the phone to her ear. "I found an apartment and it's in between campus and Grandma's house."

"What? You can't do that. We're not ready."

"I told you this is what I was going to do."

"You can't move. We don't have anyone for Grandma."

"Mom, I'm sorry, but you knew this, it isn't a surprise. You need to come and stay with her. I need a break. I need help. I'm going to have a nervous breakdown."

"No you're not."

"Mom. Listen to me. I'm taking some time to think about the apartment, but this weekend I'll be away. I need a break. I'm not coming home. So whether you come here or Mabel comes here, I will NOT be here this weekend; ALL weekend. Grandma needs someone to stay with her. Please help me."

*

Jillian packed up and said goodbye to Grandma that Saturday.

"Have fun Jillie-Bean."

"I will Grandma. I love you."

"I love you too."

Jillian walked past her parents with her bags, feeling guilty.

Her trip was well-needed. The only agenda was peace and quiet; no studying, no talking, no bathroom diaper changes. She unpacked as if she was vacationing indefinitely. Even though it was only a hotel and spa in the next town, she pretended it was somewhere far away. She unfolded a favorite photo of herself with Grandma and put it on the nightstand in the room. She gazed at it fondly. Grandma hated to have her photo taken. She never smiled. But Jillian was adamant. She would be going away to college and she wouldn't take no for an answer. The memory in the photo was that of easier times; of a love they shared and a bond that would be tested; a memory of unconditional love and mutual admiration. Jillian sighed and zipped up her suitcase.

After a late afternoon massage, she climbed into the luxurious bed, with a room service philly cheesesteak in one hand and a root beer float in the other. She wore a soft white robe, a thick towel kept her wet hair in place. She fell asleep in the middle of a chick flick and slept all the way until morning when a strip of sun peeked in. She woke up refreshed and happy. She looked at her cell phone, she had shut the ringer off. No calls, no texts. "Thank God."

She wondered how Grandma was doing. No news was a good sign she thought. And she couldn't feel badly about her decision to move, she did all she could do. She was proud that she could take care of Grandma for so long, but happy to know that she would be making the right choice in moving out to her own apartment. It was time. Wasn't it?

Her text lit up. "Call me." It was her mother's signature salutation. An abrupt call to action to command control that didn't always require urgency every single time, but Jillian called anyway.

"How's Grandma?"

"She was up all night. That monitor. We heard every noise. We had no idea."

"I told you. For a very long time I've been telling you. You didn't hear me."

"We heard you."

"You didn't *hear* me."

"We did, we just didn't understand the extent of it. When are you coming home?"

"Not until tomorrow night. I need another night."

"No."

"What do you mean, no? You don't think I deserve a break?"

"Well, your father, apparently, is just 'the guy who does the lawn now. He came inside after mowing the lawn yesterday and the sight of him made her crazy. She kept saying 'there's a stranger in the house.' Now your father has to hide from her."

"Mom, I know, but I desperately need this break. I'm not coming home tonight. You need to find someone if you're not going to be there."

On her second night away, Jillian fell asleep effortlessly, but woke in a panic around midnight to turn the phone ringer on in case they needed to reach her. Within seconds, the phone buzzed on the nightstand with her father's cell phone number. "Grandma."

Jillian lunged for the phone but couldn't muster enough breath to find her voice. Her heart pounded in her chest. She waited.

"Jillie ... "

"Yeah Dad?"

"We need you to come home. Your grandmother is sitting by the window waiting for you and she won't go to bed. It's been hours."

"I'll be right there Dad." Jillian forced her legs into her jeans, stuffed her bags, and ran down the hallway to check out. Her car sped up I-95 to the Black Rock Turnpike exit to ole' Sterner Road. She dumped her bags in the doorway.

"Hi Grandma, how are you?"

Grandma's eyes stared past her. Then she looked at her with a cordial smile and said very simply, "Good. I'm waiting for Jillian. It's late and I'm worried about her." Jillian's eyes widened. She swallowed her tears back. Her mother clutched her hands to her chest.

"Grandma, I'm Jillian. It's me."

"I don't know about that."

"OK, let's go to bed, I'll sit on the couch and wait for Jillian."

"No, it's late and she should be home by now." Then she gazed at the couch, the loveseat, and the wingback chair.

"I hate that couch."

"It's new, the other was worn, it stunk."

"It was not. I loved that couch. And this one's disgusting. It's black. What, are we living in a morgue?"

"It's navy. With pretty flowers. And we can't do anything about it now."

Grandma started to have a tantrum. Like a child, Grandma expected someone to wave a magic wand to fix things instantly. It was a fight that no one was going to win. The old furniture was long gone. She began to stare out the window again.

"Grandma, I'm Jillian. It's me." She took a photo from the console television and pointed out her portrait. "See, this is me, Jillian."

"No, I'm waiting for Jillian."

"I'm right here."

"No."

"Grandma, you have to go to bed."

"I'm not your Grandma."

"Yes. Grandma." Jillian couldn't catch her breath. Grandma always knew her. She didn't realize how painful it would be when this happened.

"I'm waiting for Jillian. Get out of my house," she screamed. "This is MY house. Get out."

"Jillian's at a sleepover," Jillian blurted out. "She won't be home tonight and we're here to stay with you. Let's get you to bed and Jillian will be here in the morning." Grandma got up and made her way to the bedroom while Jillian and her parents looked at each other shaking their heads.

"I'm sorry Jillie." Her dad put his arm around her shoulder and gave her a squeeze. "We shouldn't have called you."

"I'm sorry, I thought I could help." She leaned into his hug and wept.

"No, it's not you, not you at all, we tried. We're trying here. There's no reasoning with her. There's nothing we can do. Getting old just makes you stupid." He shook his head.

Jillian's parents left and she went upstairs for a good long cry. It was a cry for all she'd been through. A cry for what was happening to Grandma, all the memories of the past, the lost memories, the crushed hope. What about clarity and a cure? How could she have known it could get that bad. Grandma couldn't help it and she couldn't be helped. Jillian cried in defeat and guilt. Grandma needed her. She would make the decision to stay. Sean came over to rub her back and console her. He tried to stay understanding of Jillian's decision and commitment. The next morning, Jillian called the number for the cute apartment to let them know she wouldn't take it, but it was no longer available.

Chapter Twenty-Three

Months went by and Jillian *still* didn't have full-time help. "Mom, she's basically bed-ridden. She hardly gets up out of bed anymore. It is not helping her to keep her home. I can't do it even with Mabel's help. At least a convalescent home can get her up, get her moving, make her comfortable."

Her mother hadn't heard a single word. She wanted to, but her mind was elsewhere. Grandma had convinced her for years, *If you put me in a home, I'll haunt you forever.* It was a saying which her mother truly believed.

*

Eventually, Grandma stopped getting out of bed at all. Pull-ups sufficed for the bathroom routine both day and night. The need to motivate her and care for her at a medical/professional level was becoming more and more apparent. She wouldn't eat, became easily agitated, less compliant, more confused, had less moments of clarity, she was less like herself. Mom started researching nursing homes through tearful eyes, heart palpitations, and thick guilt. The wait list was long. Paperwork shuffled, phone calls were made, and several more months later, it became a reality.

*

"Right this way." A woman in scrubs and a clipboard took notes about Grandma. Her face was a blur across a desk with lots of files and paperwork. A blue crocheted doily in the shape of a starfish was placed on the corner of her desk. Jillian wondered if the crafter who made it was a patient, a friend, perhaps her own mother. Did she and her mother have a special bond? It was placed in such a way that she wondered if she had ever moved it from the spot where it was gifted originally.

"I know you want to manage this Alzheimer's," the woman said, interrupting her thoughts, directing her words toward Jillian's mother, "but what you have to realize is that Alzheimer's cannot really be managed. You can manage day to day, you can help keep someone comfortable, but Alzheimer's doesn't get better as you know. Heloise has pretty late stage Alzheimer's, so I'm sure you think you've seen it all. And I don't need to remind you that you might have the worst day yet and then the next day might be better, there may even be a glimpse of recognition. This is deceiving … dangerous, even. You think that they're getting better, and you let your guard down. Remember, there is no cure yet and until we can find a cure, it's just a cruel façade." Jillian wondered if the woman thought she was being empathetic.

"You are taking the right steps by seeking help, but there is a difference between asking for help and actually taking it. Take it. Truly take the help. Take a break. Let us help you take that break. You have worked so hard for so long to keep her in her home for what you believed to be her own best interest and we commend you for that. You've learned how to prioritize tasks, hygiene, arguments. You have kept her comfortable and safe, for as long as you were able, but her care has exceeded the usual means and that is the reason you have come to us for help. It is not selfish. It is time to take care of yourself now."

Jillian stayed silent.

"We want to make sure," the coordinator continued, "that you take that help before you get to your breaking point because that will not help anyone. She will be safe and comfortable here."

Jillian cleared her throat. "When we first put her on the list, the wait was so long and now it's already here. I didn't expect it to be this soon." Her voice was barely audible.

"You did a great job over these many months, and this is not good-bye. You can come anytime you like. But please, I urge you, take the break. Sleep without an ear out. Go to dinner without worry. You don't need to be here running yourself ragged for every meal and medicine time. We will take good care of her. That is my promise."

Blue ink scratched several papers and a long inhale and exhale filled the room. It was a silent, tear-filled ride home.

*

Jillian stepped into the doorway of Grandma's kitchen and out of habit, looked around for her, then sighed. She felt funny being in Grandma's house alone. She made her way to the loft, hearing her footsteps and the creak of the old stairs. The house was so quiet.

She took a peak around the attic space. She unhinged a rusted lunch box, packed full of doll clothes that she had made. There were bags of Cupie doll heads and bodies held closed by crusty elastic bands, boxes full of crinkled tissue paper patterns, some pinned onto colorful flowered or striped fabric, expecting to be turned into a pretty little jumper or frock. Notebooks full of written ideas, hope, creations for the next big money maker, stacks of Life and Good Housekeeping Magazines. Old luggage and bags filled with thousands of yards of fabric, for a dream that would never come to fruition, not by her own choice. It was obvious that she still pursued this passion even after Grandpa had forbidden it. In those days you "obeyed" your spouse even if he had no good reason to deny you from doing something. She never did anything with her dreams and now it was too late.

Before she left the attic space and closed the door, Jillian spotted another stack of books and magazines from long before she moved in … decades, even. They were on the topics of memory, brain games, brain food, tips for having a better memory. Jillian shook her head. "She knew this was happening to her." Jillian's eyes filled with tears and she closed the door, leaving everything back in its place.

The house felt uneasy without Grandma in it.

- Chapter Twenty - Four -

Jillian sat in the parking lot. *I wonder how many people come here and never actually go in. It's like sitting at a gravesite. Does anyone actually know I'm here?*

The security guard's metal keychain clanged as he waddled by for the third time, smiling pleasantly. He nodded his head, careful not to rush her. Jillian waited for him to pass by, clutched the steering wheel and closed her eyes tightly; tears burned the corners of her eyes. Inhaling deeply, letting the air fill her lungs to capacity until she didn't have even a fraction of space left to fill. She let it whistle out slowly through her lips as if blowing up a very large balloon, postponing the inevitable.

"Ok, I'm ready," she convinced herself out loud. She tried to turn the car off, but it wouldn't turn off. *Why can't I get the key out of the ignition?* Stepping on the brake, she tried to turn the key but ground the gears and the guard looked her way. *Car's still on. Think Jillian. Turn it off. Get out. Get out.* She quickly threw the car into park and the key slid out of the ignition effortlessly.

Walking up the sidewalk, she looked up the height of the building. The sun reflected off the windows and a trellis of cheerfully sad flowers greeted her as she wandered through. She passed people lined up in wheelchairs, baking in the sun, some looking excited to see her and genuinely disappointed when she passed by. Did they think she was there for them?

In the elevator and hallways soft churchlike music played. The combined stench of rubbing alcohol, salty boullion, mothball sweaters, and unwashed, old-people hair filled the air. Uncertainty hung around like a shriveled balloon on a string, wanting to float, but being weighed down by truth.

She walked past people sitting patiently on dusty rose-colored couches and metal folding chairs in the hallway. Geriatrics and a few young ones smiled gratefully like puppies in a window as the elevator door announced a newcomer, but sulked when the potential owner walked past them to someone else. Aides helped strap patients in wheelchairs, secure wheels, and walked residents to the dining hall. Jillian looked for room 249M. Someone sat in the hallway moaning, but no one paid attention to her. "Carly, Carly," she repeated.

A few pieces of Grandma's furniture were arranged neatly in the room. Positioned in the corner of the tiny space was her throne chair, next to that, her dresser with the wrought iron pulls. On top of the dresser were photo frames and a memory box full of trinkets, crocheting needles, yarn and pieces of fabric and letters designed to elicit some sort of memory or comfort from a place she may or may not remember as home.

Grandma stared blankly from the bed.

"Hi Grandma, it's me, Jillian."

"Jillian," she said plainly with little reaction.

"Your granddaughter."

"If you say so."

"I say so."

"Take me home." *Did she recognize me as someone from home?*

"Grandma, this is home now. You have to stay here."

"No, no, no. No, no, no, no, no."

Jillian rolled her eyes. *Was it a good idea to visit?* "Grandma, have you been eating?"

"I don't like it."

"Why don't you get something you like?"

"Who are you?"

"I'm Jillian, your granddaughter. I'm here visiting you."

"Take me home."

"I can't take you home, but maybe we can go to lunch one day, but that means you have to get out of bed, take a shower, and get dressed." One day, Jillian planned to take Grandma out to lunch. She loved Duchess on Black Rock Turnpike and that was the plan.

*

Jillian picked Grandma up for their lunch date. Grandma was clean. She didn't know how, but somehow the nurses were able to get her ready. She looked around for someone with sopping wet hair and clothes, someone who may have endured being called a jackass, maybe even someone who had been spit on, but all the nurses smiled pleasantly when Jillian passed by.

Jillian had a terrible time getting her grandmother in and out of the car and seated at a table at the restaurant. As soon as they were seated, Grandma said, "I just want to go home. Please. I just want to go home to my own house, my own things, my home." Her eyes turned sad and filled with tears. "You don't know how it is. I can't do anything. People are always telling me what to do; always in my business. They help me with everything and I can't get a moment's peace. Take me home."

Jillian stroked the top of Grandma's hand. She had forgotten how smooth and young they always were. She got lost in Grandma's words of clarity. Jillian was so eager to please this woman, and hopeful to help Grandma find happiness amidst Alzheimer's, that seeing the tears in Grandma's eyes pained her. She wanted to make it all better; spark a memory to make it all go away. She took Grandma home.

Jillian turned the key and pushed the door open for Grandma to enter. She walked into the kitchen. She looked up at the stencils she used to be so proud of painting herself. There was no recognition.

She turned to enter the living room. The red throne was missing, the spot looked bare. It was in her room at the nursing home. Grandma sat on the couch opposite the window looking displaced but she didn't know why. Jillian sat next to her in silence with a lump in her throat. Grandma sat patiently and looked around and watched Jillian watching her. The fake fruit was still on the mantle, the console tv squatted at the edge of the room with its round dials on the corner of the threadbare rug.

"We can only stay for a few more minutes, it's getting late," Jillian said as Grandma stared.

When she finally spoke, she said, "Well, what are we doing wasting time here? Where are we?" She grabbed Jillian's hand and looked her in the eyes about to cry and pleaded her point, "I don't know who you are, but I just want to go home. Can you please just take me home?"

Jillian was taken aback. Her mind raced. *Why did Alzheimer's have to steal so much? Your mind, your soul, your abilities, your personality, your you. I'm so angry right now. I'm constantly waiting for you to come back, but I have to realize that this is you now. You don't even know you. I'm sick over this. It's not fair –*

"I don't want to be here," Grandma interrupted more urgently. She started to get more agitated and upset. "Take me home." She started to sob.

"Yes, I'll take you home." Jillian was dejected, deflated. She knew Grandma would never be "home" again.

The drive "home" took minutes but felt like forever. Jillian reminisced over the familiar roads and memories of childhood in town. She pictured kids riding bikes on the sidewalks and cross-ing streets, eating ice cream cones, and pretending to be cool with their fake chocolate or bubble gum cigarettes with the puff of fake smoke, and reaching into coverall pockets to pop fun snaps at the ground to set off tiny explosions that sounded like cap guns. The sound of the pop startled her. Large drops plopped on the dusty windshield. *It wasn't supposed to rain.* She looked up.

"We're almost home." Jillian turned the wipers on which made a loud screech. The spray drenched the glass. Grandma let out a shriek and grabbed the steering wheel. The car swerved to the right, nearly side-swiping cars traveling nearby. Cars on the oppo-site side started to blow their horns to warn other cars of the crazy nut on the road. "What are you doing?" Jillian yelled. She tight-ened her grip with one hand and tried to gain control while peel-ing Grandma's fingers off of the wheel with the other. The new mist made the road slick. Jillian stomped on the brake and hopped the curb. She swerved to avoid a tree. They ended up bouncing down on the triangular green like a bocce ball. After realizing they were ok, Jillian threw her hands up in the air. "What are you thinking?" she yelled. "You could have gotten us killed."

"I want to go home."

"Yes, I gathered that. We ARE going home," Jillian yelled. "I'm bringing you home."

Jillian drove down the embankment back onto the road. Shaking. She drove the three seconds across the street to the convalescent home, Grandma's new forever home. Security helped get her out of the car and nurses helped escort her back inside.

"Did you have a good adventure?"

"You can say that again." Jillian plastered a smile on her face.

Grandma was helped back to her room where she settled in to her bed. Jillian pulled the blankets up over her and fluffed the pillow to make her comfortable. Grandma looked at her lovingly and smiled politely.

"Where's Jillian?"

Oh God.

"Can you take me home now?"

Jillian closed her eyes and nodded. She kissed Grandma on the forehead and walked out of the room in silence.

"Are you Carly?" The woman from the hallway reached her hands out, pleading.

Jillian didn't answer but kept walking. She could barely see through the tears.

*

The next time Jillian visited, she looked down the hall first to see if the Carly person was there. *Oh good she's asleep.* Jillian tiptoed past her. "Help, help. Please help me, Carly, are you Carly?"

It was constant. It didn't matter if it was day or night. "Help me," was enough to send chills down the spine and the nurses to the looney bin. With glassy eyes, the old lady reached out her knobby hands and pleaded, "Please help me, are you Carly?"

"NO?" Jillian wondered if today this would be the right answer.

The woman let out a whine which turned to a tears-and-pleading pattern, "Please help me. Carly, Carly."

Jillian winced. No wonder her family had to put her somewhere, not knowing how to make it better. "Are you Carly?"

"Yes, yes, I'm Carly, Shhhh, be quiet," Jillian lied.

"Shhhh," the woman started to shush back loudly.

"Be quiet, what do you need?"

"You shush, be quiet."

"What do you need?"

The woman paused to think a moment. She inhaled to speak and when she opened her mouth she whined loudly, "Please help me. Carly, Carly." *Oh God.*

*

And one day the woman was gone. There was no explanation. She wasn't in the hallway, her room was cleaned out, and no one spoke of her again.

*

As the months went on, Grandma was becoming increasingly agitated; more easily agitated than usual. On a bad day Jillian's visit would trigger fits of anger, she would hit and spit at her nurses, and say she wanted to go "home" all day long. On the good days, the nurses would find her smiling politely in the lunch hall watching and nodding her head, the only form of participation in a senior environment she'd ever allowed. One couldn't predict which way the mood would lead from day to day or minute to second for that matter. On particularly bad days the nurses administered morphine or medical marijuana. On these days she could be found drooling, face swollen, slumped in her chair like a stroke victim. This wasn't her either. Jillian and her mother began to work together to fight for other treatments.

Jillian started to visit less. It agitated Grandma to try to figure out who she was, and it broke Jillian's heart that Grandma didn't know her. There was no conversation that could cure or comfort.

*

Eventually, Grandma couldn't form words, she spoke jibberish. The nurses couldn't get her up out of bed and her brain forgot to tell her how to do simple things like eat. She was moved to a different floor with constant care, but Jillian knew this transition was actually called "Hospice". Her skin became jaundiced; she was starving to death. Because it was decided to keep her comfortable but not to resuscitate (DNR), it was a slow, barbaric, cruel process in Jillian's mind. There was nothing peaceful or natural about it.

Animals go through less pain when there's no hope of recovery. There's nothing humane about keeping her hanging on. She'd have a whole lot to say about this if she could.

As the days went on, her breathing was labored. She was hardly anything more than skin and bones. She couldn't hear anything. She slept most of the time and didn't know anyone was around. She had no idea what was going on around her.

It became increasingly obvious that it was the end and equally hard to witness. The family gathered in her room; aunts, uncles, cousins, family who hadn't shown up to help over the last few years made an appearance.

Conversations went on around her bedside as if she wasn't even there.

Jillian's mother asked, "Do you think she knows we're all here?"

"Yes, I know you're all here." Grandma's eyes sprang open. The room gasped and went silent.

"Grandma … you can hear us?" Jillian asked.

She nodded.

"Did someone clean out your hearing aid?" Jillian joked. No one laughed.

Grandma smiled and looked around.

They all looked at each other. She hadn't been responsive in a conversation in months and definitely couldn't hear. It didn't make sense. Jillian couldn't help but look around to see if she could see Grandma's spirit floating in the room somewhere. It could be the only logical explanation if Grandma's body was in the bed, but her spirit was sitting in the chair watching everyone and listening. It was a gift. They say that happens.

"Where's Patti?"

"I'm here."

Everyone cleared the room and they had their private time together. Jillian could only assume she wanted to tell her goodbye and got a bit jealous. *Does she know she's not really family?* Jillian could see how relaxed Grandma was after Patti told her that everyone would be okay after she passed and everyone left that night with a slightly calmer mind, except Jillian. She couldn't say goodbye.

"Grandma, I'll be back tomorrow," Jillian whispered.

She wrote a poem that night.

Your Last of Days

You took care of me
Now I'll take care of you.
Put your trust in me
I am here for you.

It's me who you know
Though you're not too sure.
Put faith in my smile
Even though it's a blur.

Holding your hand
Sitting by your side
Looking at your pain
As you hide it with pride.

All your prayers are heard
Your wishes are all planned.
So please don't worry
There is not one loose end.

So breathe now in ease
Know that we'll be fine
Finding strength somehow
In each little sign.

Know that you are loved
In these your last of days.
And know that I am here
For now, then, and always.

*

Jillian was ready to leave the house the next morning when her mother called. All she heard from the other end was, "She died."

"What?"

"She died."

"Okay," was all she could muster.

She hung up the phone and wailed. She couldn't catch her breath. She grabbed tissues out of the box one at a time. She used them all at once in a big wad. She left the house in a daze. She drove all over the road, getting lost, taking wrong turns. She could barely see. She didn't even know how she got to the convalescent home.

When she got off the elevator a nurse quickly linked her arm and escorted her down the hall, bombarding her with condolences. Jillian didn't make it into the room, she stopped short in the doorway and gasped. An odor hit her that was a putrid mixture of antiseptic and something unknown. She didn't comprehend who else was in the room, she only saw Death and couldn't take her eyes off of it. She had never seen Death before and it wasn't at all what she had imagined. It didn't look peaceful. It looked horrific. Still ... This wasn't Grandma. It was a cadaverous yellow body in a bed where Grandma used to lie. The eyes were sunken skeletal sockets and the head was tilted back. The mouth was open wide like the pictures she had seen of people caught in the lava in Pompeii, gasping for breath, crying out from pain, dying alive.

It was the first time Jillian had doubt with a punishing, critical self-guilt about all that she had been taught to believe in Catholicism. There were no angels, there was no music, no peace, no spiritual feeling. It felt empty ... quiet, but uneasy. Grandma was there, but she wasn't there. *Is God here? Is God with her somewhere else?* He didn't seem to be surrounding them in love and shielding Jillian from her doubts. *Where is He?* Jillian looked around for answers. *Oh my God ... there's no God. There's no heaven. Two decades of forced Catholicism to learn that there was only one way to believe. God is in Heaven. Jesus died for our sins. If God is real, why would he make people suffer? Why would God do that to her? Why did he let her suffer if He is so Good? Why can we credit God for all the things in life that happens that are good? This is horrific. God works in mysterious ways. This is not God.* Never had Jillian questioned it until then.

Why she had believed in God? Why had she gone to mass all these years? Was it obligatory habit rather than desire? Old priests preached about abstinence and fidelity while she and her boyfriend counted the minutes for the forty-five minute mass to be over. A condom wrapper pulled out of his pocket instead of a single for the donation basket. The parishioners pretended not to know that the priest had to be driven home from the Irish pub the night before and may not have even been to bed yet. All discrepancies surfaced. She lost her faith instantly.

*

Jillian studied the stained glass on each of the windows just a few short days later. She'd grown up in that particular church but had never really paid attention to the story behind each scene on the panes. The smell of incense burned her throat. She tried to clear it. She grabbed the podium and inhaled. "I'm finding this insurmountable ..." she began. "Years of grieving cannot prepare you for the moment it actually happens. You expect closure; finally an end to the grief because you think you've already grieved, but it brings up a whole new set of emotions, thoughts, regrets ... memories. You think that now you can relax, they're in a better place, you've done all you could do, but a small piece of your heart is irreparable, you can't help thinking that maybe something could have been changed, or fixed. But now I know that it cannot. Not now anyway." She looked over at the casket.

She stopped to dab her nose and continued. "Grandma and I were best friends; we shared secrets. We genuinely loved each other. She would paint my nails in bright red and make my favorite foods; Pierogies with lots of butter and onions, or cheese blintzes, or stuffed cabbage. She used to tell me stories about hanging laundry together with Eleanor Roosevelt. They had adjacent yards back in the day." Jillian shrugged her shoulders, not quite knowing if this was true or made up. "She told me they would have conversations while they collected berries from the bushes in the yard." A low murmur blanketed the folding seats that were lined up just behind the wingback chairs in the front row of the chapel.

"Eventually, Alzheimer's started to take over her brain and body, but worse than that, she knew it. But anyone who came over to visit her would have known that. When she would get frustrated or forget something simple, she would knock her index finger into the side of her head and say, 'BING, pick up the marbles'." It prompted a nervous giggle from the family. "I ... I just can't... I just can't believe this is it." Jillian's voice squeaked. She lowered her head down and began to sob. She could hear the chatter start and the family rushed in to swoop her away. She felt like she was drowning in a crowd of arms touching her, people grabbing her, pulling her to safety, but all she wanted was to stay there with Grandma where she belonged. Jillian knew it would be the last time to be with her. *How dare they? I need more time with her. How could this be it? Why is everyone rushing me? I'm not ready.*

Jillian was escorted with wrenching heartbreak down the aisle in the opposite direction from Grandma. *I need more time!* They stopped her right in front of Jillian's mother and they were forced to look each other in the eye. Her mother approached her. "I'm sorry." She said

"I'm sorry, too." Jillian said. She felt her mother's arms around her briefly. Her dad was next in line.

Jillian spotted Sean waiting for her. The tears in his eyes matched hers.

Chapter Twenty-Five

The moments that followed the funeral were a blur. Jillian turned the key to Grandma's house, took a deep breath, and gave herself the courage to proceed. She scanned past a small statue of Jesus on the cross by the front door just before the entrance to the living room. Under Jesus was a yellow-stained plastic bowl and inside, a crusty cube that once was a sponge to soak the holy water. Jillian only remembers Grandma dipping her finger in and making the sign of the cross once or twice in her lifetime. She looked in toward the living room where fake fruit still sat in a bowl on the mantle. Even though Grandma hadn't lived in the house for several months, Jillian still looked for her. She wanted to feel her presence. "Grandma" she whispered, willing her to answer. The house was cold. Still. "Are you here?" Nothing.

*

Jillian began to fall back into the pace of real life, but occasionally memories would flood her vision. Sean knew she needed time to wallow. She'd been so strong since the funeral. He fixed her a cup of tea, ran a nice hot tub with Epsom salt, lit candles, turned the lights off and put music on. He kissed her gently on the forehead and gave her the time she needed.

She slid in the relaxing bath and welcomed the memories that she'd been trying so hard to block out. She thought about how she did everything she could to keep Grandma home; her fits, her confusion, her agonizing bath time, the bath bench with a towel wrapped around her, frightened. She thought about how Grandma smiled at the comfort of the warm washcloth on her neck followed by hitting, spitting and screaming '911'. Jillian shook her head. *You can come in. I fed the goat today. Get down here, quick, there's a bear. I was engaged once. The bus picked us up and brought us to a party. I closed the account. I want to go home, take me home. I'm waiting for Jillian. Grandma, it's me. BING! I can't do this anymore. Things don't always turn out the way we plan.*

Jillian pressed her fingers over her watery eyes allowing the warmth to soothe her. She inhaled deeply, exhaling in choppy bursts, not sure if she wanted to let it all out or stay calm. But her body began to shake. She nodded her head and tried to breathe. "Grandma, where are you? I miss you so much." Jillian shook her head. "You didn't deserve what happened to you. It was so difficult. But I want you to know that the hardest times were not when you were hitting me or pulling my hair." Jillian swallowed to continue, "I know you didn't mean it. The hardest times were in your moments of clarity when you knew what was happening to you. And it broke my heart for you." Jillian could barely speak above a whisper. She closed her eyes and let the floodgates open. "You're at peace now and you don't have to worry. Sean will take care of me. We're planning on getting married. I wish you could see me walk down the aisle; hold my children." She sobbed loudly until there were no more tears left.

*

Jillian reached for the apartment listings on the dresser and held it to her chest. She climbed into bed with it and looked around the loft before turning off the light. Just inside that closet were the necessities for her new life; the heart trivet, the utensils, the plates.

Before she dozed off she whispered, "Grandma, are you here?" She fell asleep without an answer.

Grandma's Spirit (From the Author)

After Grandma died, I thought it would be easy to write her story, but it was just as painful to re-live it as it was to go through it the first time. I wanted Grandma's Alzheimer's to be portrayed as a positive story about love, support, and the funny things that happened along the way, but this was more difficult than I had expected. This was personal, emotional, special, draining, and stressful all wrapped into one. Grandma flit in and out of a world of unexplained strangeness that was difficult to fathom, but I wanted to stay true to the spirit and feistiness that was Grandma. It took me several years to be able to capture her spirit on paper.

*

On the day that I completed writing the last word of this book, I closed my laptop proudly, and proceeded with my schedule as if it was any other regular day. Grandma's story was a real labor of love. As I drove, a puffy white cloud formed in the sky in the shape of a smile complete with parentheses-style cartoon cheeks. The emoji filled the sky. I couldn't believe my eyes. It was perfectly placed in the middle of Route Eight, and I had no other option than to notice it. *Thank you Grandma!* Within seconds, the smile turned into a heart. And that's how I knew I'd accomplished something wonderful in Grandma's honor.

The End.

Acknowledgements

Thank you to my wonderful husband, Erick, for your encouragement and support while I relived this Alzheimer's story. These memories came to me as clearly as the moment they happened. Had I allowed you to read the book along the way, you would have understood my moods.

Thank you to my children Kaitlyn, Brendan, and now Daniel, and Abby, for understanding that my eight o'clock hour is sacred writing time. I love you all.

Thank you to my parents who made my living arrangements with Grandma possible. I had special moments with her that I cherish. Also, thank you for understanding that although many of the experiences in the book happened, this book is also a work of fiction. *Embellishment is part of being an author.*

Thank you to Grandma for teaching me courage, persistence, humor, resilience, and for the little signs I've learned to acknowledge.

Thank you to my friend and photographer Tracy Weed. You helped bring Grandma's essence to life with this amazing cover photo. Thank you for your encouragement during the writing of some of the hardest parts of this book.

Thank you to my beta readers and the following people who took the time to give me suggestions, feedback, and encouragement along the way: John Bates, Dawn Costantiello, Ann Sovak, Kathryn Harrison, Dayna Steele, and of course, Karen Gamble, for her amazing book review, hope, and found friendship on Twitter.

Lastly, but most importantly, thank you to my Editor, Natalie Bates, for pushing me to go deeper, encouraging me, and always believing in me. You have helped make this book a reality! I look forward to working with you again!

Resources

- 10 Signs of Alzheimer's : www.alz.org/10signs
  - Alzheimer's Foundation: www.alzfdn.org
  - Mayo Clinic Overview: http://www.mayoclinic.org/diseases-conditions/alzheimers-disease/home/ovc-20167098
  - For the people helping people with Alzheimer's: https://alzheimers.acl.gov/
  - Alzheimer's support and education workshops: http://www.alz.org/cwva/in_my_community_education.asp

Books

- Blue Hydrangeas by Marianne Sciucco
- Chicken Soup for the Soul Living with Alzheimer's & Other Dementias: 101 Stories of Caregiving, Coping, and Compassion Kindle Edition by Amy Newmark
- Surviving Alzheimers' with Friends, Facebook, and a Really Big Glass of Wine by Dayna Steele
- Alzheimer's Daughter by Jean Lee
- Still Alice by Lisa Genova
- Weeds in Nana's Garden by Kathryn Harrison
- What's Happening to Grandpa by Maria Shriver
- The Notebook by Nicholas Sparks

Movies

- Still Alice (Julianne Moore)
- Iris (Judi Dench)
- The Notebook (Gena Rowlands)

Essays

Through the Doors by Fran Cusworth

What People are Saying about Lost Memories Found Hope

"Each family member copes with Alzheimer's in their own way: denial, grief, acceptance, and avoidance.

Michelle Spray leads us through the realities of the "long goodbye," from unplugging the stove, taking away the car keys, asking for help, and eventually finding a nursing home. Her main character, Jillian, bears the burden of caring for her grandmother who has the disease.

Written with humor and love, Spray deftly paints a portrait of a young woman facing these challenges with equal measures of grace and despair. I highly recommend this book for anyone who has walked alongside a loved one with Alzheimer's." – Karen Gamble

About the Author

Michelle Spray is an additional needs mom living in Connecticut with her husband and their blended family. She is currently writing about her family's bravery throughout health issues and a sequel to Life's Reason's (Introspective Poetry and Short Stories). Michelle is proud to supply an underlying theme of hope and inspiration in all of her books.

You can find Michelle's other books on:
Amazon: www.amazon.com/author/michellespray

Facebook: www.facebook.com/SprayBooksEtc
Instagram: www.instagram.com/SprayBooksEtc
Twitter: www.twitter.com/SprayBooksEtc

SNEAK PEEK

Life's Reasons by Michelle Spray

Introspective Poetry and Short Stories

Tiny Angels

You deteriorated slowly and sadness grew. Your painful expressions tore the heart apart. You whisprered to be heard.

Your immobile body was not deserved. You struggled to overcome the obstacles.

Upon permission, your muscles finally relaxed. Your breathing calmed until it ceased. Silence filled the room. Tears fell, but the struggle was over.

It was fairly warm outside the day we gathered to say good-bye, yet it began to snow. The snowflakes flittered around us like tiny angels. Comforting. Graceful. And as the birds flew up into the sky, the tiny angels rested on their wings to look down on us … forever.

www.amazon.com/author/michellespray
www.facebook.com/SprayBooksEtc
www.MichelleSpray.com

Life's Reasons by Michelle Spray
Introspective Poetry and Short Stories

In the Wings

Sadness is the loneliness you feel
when someone close to you dies.
The memories cloud your head
And the happy times you have shared surround you.
The tears seem to fall from nowhere.

Sometimes the sad memories fight for the spotlight,
but the happy memories are always waiting in the wings
to take their place.

At the end of the performance,
the last sigh of accomplishment is expelled.
The dusty curtain closes in.
The orchestra of angels relieve the pain
and the stage fright is over.

Following the exit comes previously unheard compliments and
praise. The flowers and cards are given graciously. The performance will always be remembered by all who were inspired, in the
audience and in the wings.

www.amazon.com/author/michellespray
www.facebook.com/SprayBooksEtc
www.MichelleSpray.com

SNEAK PEEK

Life's Reasons by Michelle Spray

Introspective Poetry and Short Stories

Bubble Wonder

So fascinating, so amazing
Mesmerizing to a child

Chase it
Poke it
It pops.

Little ones,
High ones,
Laughter

Follow it until...
it floats out of reach.

Pop!

Possibilities.

www.amazon.com/author/michellespray
www.facebook.com/SprayBooksEtc
www.MichelleSpray.com

Life's Reasons by Michelle Spray
Introspective Poetry and Short Stories

That Way Again

Swinging on a rope swing
Climbing up to the tree house
Secrets between friends
Laughter 'til dawn

Running through puddles
Chasing a butterfly
Blowing big bubbles
High into the sky

Dust from an old mitt
Catching a baseball
Jumping through sprinklers
Eating a cone

Learning a new game
Searching for fun times
Singing out loudly
Even off-key

Question after question
Wondering how life works
Overly honest
And growing by leaps

Carefree and hopeful
Unhardened by wisdom
Could we look back and
Live that way again?

www.amazon.com/author/michellespray
www.facebook.com/SprayBooksEtc
www.MichelleSpray.com